the San Franciscan

A Love Story In a Time of War

Florence Gold

Azalea Art Press
Berkeley, California

ISBN: 978-0-9849760-5-8

To Bob, without whom this book
would not have been written—
and finished—and for his understanding,
encouragement and advice.

ACKNOWLEDGEMENTS

I wish to express my appreciation to the following sources of historical information:

Los Angeles, A Sunset Pictorial, Sunset Books.
Los Angeles 200: A Bicentennial Celebration, by Art Seidenbaum and John Malmin.
The National Geographic Magazine, June 1943.
This Fabulous Century 1930-1940, Time-Life Books.
This Fabulous Century, 1940-1950, Time-Life Books.
Naval History, by Admiral Morrow.
Pacific Islands Year Book, 1944.
San Francisco As It Is, As It Was, by Paul C. Johnson and Richard Reinhardt.
World War II, by Brigadier Peter Young.
Yesterday's Los Angeles, by Norman Dash.

Portions of the following songs were used in my novel: "They're Either Too Young or Too Old" and "When the Lights Go On Again All Over the World."
My gratitude also goes out to:
Merlin Meyer, Bureau of Labor Statistics.
Hotel Employees and Restaurant Employees Union Local 483; the Fairmont Hotel, San Francisco, California; and especially to the many Navy veterans who were willing to share their memories.

Special thanks to Diane Swanson, for her suggestions and encouragement; and most of all to Robert S. Gold, for his memories, his proofreading and his patience.

This novel is a work of fiction. Names, characters, places and incidents are either the product of the author's imagination or are used fictitiously. Any resemblance to actual events, locales or persons, living or dead, is entirely coincidental.

Although the author was as accurate as she could be in recounting the historical events referred to in these pages, the actual timing was occasionally changed to coincide with the fictional story. The events and characters, other than those historical events and characters, are purely fiction, of course.

INTRODUCTION

My mother, Florence Gold, was passionate about reading and writing. As a young San Franciscan, she read everything she could get her hands on, including her brother Phil's chemistry books. She would often read a book or more a day, and she loved to read out loud. She read to my sister and I every school day when we came home for lunch. My mother read to us while we were traveling with my father in the car, and continued to do this long after my parents' retirement. She was such a good reader, that I felt as if I had read the books myself.

Her love of writing also began in childhood. After my parents moved to a retirement community, I had the sad task of emptying their home. This ended up being a surprising and privileged process, as I discovered things about my parents that I had not known. I found boxes of my Mother's writings—poems, short stories, and several novels, thousand of written pages—spanning her entire life. I got to know my mother in a different way, not as a parent, but as someone whom I admired and of whom I was proud.

It gives me great pleasure to see one of her stories published. Her dream of becoming a published author has become a reality and this was perhaps her greatest wish. I hope you get to know her, and enjoy her story.

- Stephen Gold
2012

PROLOGUE

The many planes of the Japanese Armada took off from their carriers, armed and ready. As they approached their target, the pilots were listening to the sweet strains of Harry Owens' Hawaiian music from Honolulu, a melody anyone with a radio could hear. Then slowly, plane-by-plane, they soared off, honing in on that very radio beam to make their bombing run on Pearl Harbor.

And then, on December 7, 1941, it was a time of war.

CHAPTER 1

They were seated in the Japanese Tea Garden, waiting for the kimono-clad waitresses to notice them.

"It's supposed to be called the Chinese Tea Garden now, you know," she murmured. "Because of the war."

"Yes, I know," Michael Stratton replied in the same low tone. "I can't get used to it, can you? It just doesn't seem right somehow."

"I know." She nodded in complete understanding.

"I had some Nisei buddies in high school. They told me an old Japanese named—what was it—Hagiwara, that was it, Makoto Hagiwara—actually started it, but they have been placed . . ." He stopped suddenly, embarrassed.

Again she nodded. This was especially hard for Ruth Braunstein to comprehend. According to the newspapers, the Germans were putting all the Jews in their country and those they conquered into concentration camps, which were supposed to be horrible. Some rumors actually had it that they were even killed there. She shuddered. And this was her own country. Our own people couldn't be doing that to the Japanese, could they? They didn't do it to the Italians or the Germans. It just couldn't be only because of the difference in the shape of their eyes. It didn't make sense. And she couldn't bear to think of her own government in the same class as the Nazis.

"Yes, I've heard they've been placed in—in camps, too. I don't understand it at all," she responded. "I just know it isn't right, and yet I'm an American, of course! I feel like I'm a traitor to speak against my own country, but—I just don't understand it."

"Neither do I," Michael said. He straightened his Navy cap. "Look, honey, I'm fighting for my country, though I haven't really been in the fighting yet. But I probably will. And there's a good chance I'll fight the Japs even though I can't really understand what we're doing and why we're doing it. Those were good Japanese buddies I had in high school. Nothing wrong with them. And they've been moved too."

"Oh, I can't stand the thought of it," Ruth lamented. He put his hand reassuringly on hers.

"At least I know they're not killing them, not the American-born ones, anyway. They're different from those dirty Japs who bombed Pearl Harbor while pretending to be so cozy with us here. Those are the ones we're really fighting."

The Chinese waitress approached to take their order and their conversation ceased. As Michael ordered jasmine tea and fortune cookies for two, he looked again at Ruth and thought of her mother. Although she didn't resemble Mrs. Braunstein in appearance, the warmth and kindness that emanated from her was the same. He had been impressed, despite himself, when he picked up Ruth and was introduced to her mother—not by her clothes or appearance certainly, but by her controlled friendliness and wary acceptance of him.

He had to admit to himself that the thought had occurred to him that Ruth's family would be overjoyed that a man of his social standing, the son of one of the first families of San Francisco, was taking her out. Mrs. Braunstein, however, had the attitude that she was reluctantly entrusting a rare jewel to his care and he had better return it safe and undamaged. She had also managed to convey the kindly concern she apparently felt for all humanity, that she even cared what happened to him. Somehow, though they really weren't alike, Mrs. Braunstein reminded him of Bridget, their Irish maid, who had been more of a mother to him than his own. Mrs. Braunstein, though rather aloof, was a bit more dignified than Bridget, but they seemed like kindred spirits.

Ruth was aware of Michael's scrutiny, and she looked down to hide the satisfaction in her eyes. She knew she looked her very best, even down to the real nylon stockings (her only pair) that she had waited in a block-long line to buy. Even though they were baggy and she could never get the seams absolutely straight, the nylons were better than that brown leg paint that streaked orange in the rain. Since silk was impossible to obtain and Japan was the only source, she felt lucky that at least they used a small part of the supply of nylon to make stockings as well as parachutes.

Her beige suit, with its peplum jacket, together with the matching brown alligator shoes (she just loved her shoes!) and bag, might have been a little dressy for the Japanese Tea Garden, but she wore no hat or gloves, which made her outfit more casual. Of course, if she'd known they were going to dinner, she would have worn her beige hat with the large pink cabbage roses and her brown leather gloves, also trimmed in alligator.

Even if he took her to dinner later, however, she was dressed nicely enough to overlook the usual accessories. Her heart warmed toward her mother, as she recalled how she had given her only daughter her only ration ticket for the shoes. Ruth had spent her own ticket almost immediately, and she hadn't asked her mother for hers, assuming that she would want to use it for herself. But her mother had insisted, saying that it would just go to waste if Ruth didn't use it. Actually, the ration tickets for the shoes were harder to come by than the money to buy them!

She leaned over the tiny table to pour a cup of tea for Michael from the pretty little teapot, and then disaster struck. She felt the hook and eye separate in the back of her garter belt. She had always worn it over her panties, seeing no reason to put it underneath. She now saw a reason.

The bathroom in the Garden, which was a poor one at best, was at the entrance. The teahouse was in the back. How was she going to make it all the way back to the entrance with her stockings and garter belt trailing along the floor?

If Michael wondered at Ruth's sudden hurry to finish the tea and cookies, he gave no sign. They chatted away about this and that, though Ruth seemed somewhat preoccupied.

When they stood up, Ruth made it a point to take small steps, keeping her legs together to keep the garter belt as high as possible. She was aware that the stockings already bagging alarmingly below her knees. Then they came to the stairs leading out of the teahouse. She hesitated. She had no choice. She walked up the stairs, losing ground with every step.

They made their way to the observation deck above the teahouse, which overlooked one of the lovely little man-made lakes in the Garden. It was usually Ruth's favorite spot. Water lilies dotted the lake, and the beautiful Koi, some golden, some multicolored, swam in and around them. Graceful green trees and bushes encircled the lake. The Garden was large enough to stroll through on a lazy afternoon, but, in true Japanese fashion, was miniaturized to give the impression of much more space. Ruth often said that she recharged her soul in that tranquility. Her soul was not in trouble at that time, however. She needed other help. Looking about desperately, she saw no one else at the moment in that area. Also, there was a small bush near the archway leading to the bridge that afforded a minimum amount of privacy, at least behind her if she backed up.

Michael was commenting on the fact that he had never been in the Garden when the cherry blossoms were in bloom and that this was no exception. He gazed down at the Koi swimming below them, admiring their brilliant hues. He didn't seem to notice the ever-increasing ballooning of Ruth's stockings, which kept pace with the ever-deepening misery on her face.

"Michael," she began hesitantly.

"Hmmm?" He was looking at the lake with appreciation, noting once again how artistically the water lilies were placed in the lake. The effect was so pleasing.

"Michael," she was as matter-of-fact as she could manage. "I'm having some trouble with my stockings, and—they're falling down." She now spoke as quickly as she could. Michael, astounded at this peculiar statement, nevertheless kept his gaze gallantly on the lake, centering his eyes on a very large golden Koi as it swam majestically below. "Michael, would you please keep looking that way until I make repairs? I can't wait for—for more privacy."

"Certainly, Ruth." He was amused as well as shocked. His mother, of course, would have thought this to be scandalously wanton and bold. But Ruth was obviously not flaunting her sensuality. She was plain miserable and that accounted for her strange behavior at the teahouse. He lost sight of the large fish, which had darted off into the depths, and stared at the far side of the lake, keeping his eyes forward.

Ruth valiantly backed up to the bush, hitched up her skirt and her slip in the back, grabbed the offending garter belt, now around her knees, and hooked it up again. It took longer than usual with her shaking hands, and the leaves on the bush scratched her generous buttocks, but no one else appeared, and Michael was a perfect gentleman. She couldn't tell if her seams were straight or not, but that was a minor consideration. That she could fix in that miserable bathroom.

She joined him at the bridge.

"I'm so sorry," she mumbled, terribly embarrassed. What must he think of her? Then she looked up at him. He was trying not to laugh.

"It wasn't funny," she began, indignant.

He lost the battle and began to laugh uproariously, holding onto the railing for support. "Sorry," he managed to get out. "But it really is . . ." and off he went again.

She couldn't help it. She began to laugh, too. "I guess it really is funny, after all," she giggled. Then, so he wouldn't think something worse had happened (after all, she wasn't losing her panties, was she?), she tried to explain the loss of the garter belt. The more she tried to explain, the more he laughed. With a few more shame-faced giggles and a great sense of relief that apparently he didn't think the worse of her, she took his arm and they strolled off the deck.

With a twinkle in his eye, he asked her if she felt like walking up The Bridge to Heaven, which went almost straight up and down with small footholds along each side, or if it would mean the loss of anything else. She gave him a good-natured slap on his arm, and he laughed.

"I haven't been on that since I was a child," she smiled. "Now, with high heels and all," and she laughed herself at the "all", "I don't think I'd better try."

"I have to agree with you," he responded gravely, and they went into paroxysms again.

He showed how athletic he was by passing all the children on the high bridge, standing on the top like Tarzan of the Apes, and coming down just a bit more cautiously. She clapped her delight on the sidelines and privately determined that, in the future, she would wear her garter belt inside her panties.

Time passed too quickly, and it was soon the hour for Michael to take Ruth home to her waiting parents. She couldn't help thinking that in spite of her mishap, she'd had a wonderful time, and that if it hadn't been for this terrible war, she probably would never have met him.

CHAPTER 2

She hated the news and listened to it as seldom as possible, but today she was home alone. She turned the knob on the small, wooden cathedral-shaped radio.

She couldn't quite believe it, but somehow she knew this was really it. As she passed through the kitchen, the announcer's voice changed from his usually dulcet tone to one of alarm. "Pearl Harbor has just been attacked by the Japanese," he practically shouted. "We're at war!"

When her parents arrived home, she told them the news, but neither one could believe it, either. She walked down to the corner store three blocks away to get a paper to prove it, but once she entered the small "mama-papa" store, she realized the papers wouldn't be printed until later that day, so she returned home without asking anyone else. She was shy and she didn't want to risk further skepticism.

When the news broke into the regular broadcasting, she was the first at the Philco, even before her parents. They were shocked and somewhat subdued about it. But for Ruth, just eighteen, there was an inner excitement—she was actually living through history in the making. She was an intelligent young woman, and she knew men would die and suffer, possibly even her own brothers, but she was excited. This was the first taste of real life she had had, and she recognized when it touched her.

Ruth had lived with her parents all her eighteen years in the Richmond, a middle-class district in the city of San Francisco, where the blue Pacific Ocean was in their backyard. Her parents had always called the modest rented flat they lived in, "one of those modern cracker boxes that just wasn't built well like the old houses." The thought did occur to her to leave them and set up her own apartment, but she didn't have the nerve. In 1941 the only justification for a young woman to leave her parents before marriage was either a knock-down, drag-out fight and estrangement or the disgrace of becoming a "fallen woman." She satisfied herself with threatening to leave whenever wills clashed. She had applied at The White House, the elegant downtown department store, for a job right after she graduated from high school in June, and she was now a full-fledged saleswoman, so she was financially independent. Ruth was very fair, however, and she decided on her own that $40 a month room and board was quite adequate to pay her parents. It took quite a chunk out of the total $125 a month she was paid by the store. Her parents were surprised and not altogether pleased, but they took the money, believing it was good for her character.

She had spent much of her childhood in the hospital, in a convalescent home, in bed. Rheumatic fever had invaded her body when she was nine, frightening her and her family terribly. It was the middle of the Great Depression, and there was no medical insurance and no money for medical care. The people at the clinic were kind, but they were busy and had no time for the emotional needs of a nine-year-old girl. They saved her life, which was in doubt for a time, and they were satisfied, though she was left with what was called "a heart condition." She was also left with a fear of rejection, a fear of new experiences, and a fear of people, with whom she was shy and sometimes inadvertently rude. She didn't know how to relate to them, not having had sufficient practice. She preferred the world of her books to the real world.

She would always remember the doctor saying to her mother, right in front of her as if she were not there, that she could never lead a normal life and might not even live to adulthood. That memory stayed in the back of her mind where it wouldn't bother her. She had learned to live with it.

The war years opened up a new world. The USO, the Hospitality House or "Hop House," the attitude that all soldiers were to be reasonably indulged, "for tomorrow we die," plunged her into a giddy social life. For one who had scarcely been to a party before, the atmosphere was dangerous. She was attractive when she smiled. So often before she had been sullen, because she was afraid of people—afraid they wouldn't like her. Afraid of rejection, she rejected people first.

Her figure, with her 38-inch bust, was more than noticeable, however. As a teenager, she had learned to conceal it, in embarrassment. Now she was learning to reveal it instead. She learned to apply makeup, a bit too much at first, and she tried to learn to walk tall. That was difficult, since she was just a bit over five feet three inches tall, and she still looked down at her toes when she walked. But her attitude subtly changed, and she took delight in the fact that she was someone who was attractive to men. When she dressed to go out to the USO dance every Saturday night and examined herself critically in the mirror, she wasn't too dissatisfied. She couldn't do anything about the freckles on her nose, but with her red hair and large, expressive green eyes, big bosom, tiny waist and legs that weren't too bad, she would not pass unnoticed at the USO. Her hips were her biggest problem—they were just too generous.

She was unbelievably naïve, however. Perhaps that was her protection and her appeal. She favored the Navy men and she learned rather quickly how to kiss. Her parents, of course, had never kissed her on the mouth; and, after her first kiss, she thought she might be pregnant until her best friend, Sally Simpson, told her the true facts of life. She progressed rapidly to necking, which she enjoyed thoroughly. She kept her virginity, though just barely, because it was most important to her parents and because she was afraid, though tempted.

She was ready.

She met Michael in April of 1942, when the war, which was supposed to be over in a few weeks, seemed to be lasting forever. It was her usual Saturday night at the USO, and she had attended, as usual, with Sally, a tall slender brunette with long flowing hair and great legs. Sally was a more conservative dresser than Ruth, and considerably more sophisticated. She was approved of, more generally, by the Senior Hostesses. Attractive, smart-looking rather than pretty, Sally's taste in men differed dramatically from Ruth's, and the boys who found her attractive were not attracted to Ruth, which was one of the reasons for their long friendship. They had known each other since grammar school days, since before Ruth fell ill. Sally was the only visitor she had outside of her family when she was confined to bed. There wasn't much about each other that they didn't know.

Ruth had been called in by a supervising Senior Hostess to be once again chastised for her low-cut blouse and short skirt. "Do you know what you look like?" the older woman, whom Ruth knew as Mrs. Stratton, asked severely. "You look like a chorus girl in that!" Ruth looked her in the eye, rebellious but not too belligerent, for she didn't want to be barred from the club, thinking that she rather liked looking like a chorus girl. Taking the remark as a compliment rather than an insult softened Ruth's attitude, and she exerted herself to be more pleasant to the supervising hostess, who, however, became more incensed than ever. The fact that she was thought to be "fast" pleased Ruth, because she enjoyed shocking her elders, and partially because it seemed glamorous and unobtainable to her.

She left Mrs. Stratton as soon as she could, with both ladies knowing that no change would be made in her dress. Mrs. Stratton, shaking her head after Ruth left, found her obvious sensuality trashy and disapproved whole-heartedly of her and her provocative dress. Only Ruth knew that her dress merely indicated the role she was playing and that she had never taken that irrevocable step.

When Michael cut in on her on the dance floor, chemistry seemed to flow between them. She couldn't keep up her act of "party girl," and she behaved naturally—shy and entranced by Michael's rugged good looks. She didn't know how much more attractive that was. Her eyes brightened, and her entire being unconsciously became warmer and softer, yet more animated. She was with him for only a few moments, just long enough for them to exchange first names and silently confirm their mutual attraction, when they were cut in on. She immediately became the professional hostess again, disappointed as she was. Michael cut in on her once more, and she knew then that this was special. When, once again, a stranger interfered, this time she was quiet and sullen, looking for Michael over the young man's shoulder. She had never been this popular, she thought bitterly—not now, not now!

Michael tried to cut in once more, but he had become impatient and frustrated. "Look, honey—this is not good. Isn't there someplace we can be alone?"

Suddenly Ruth was afraid. She was afraid of what might happen and she was afraid of what might not happen.

"We're not allowed to go home with the boys," she responded primly, looking down. "It's against the rules." Though she was usually honest to a fault, Ruth didn't want to mention how often she disobeyed the rules when she didn't agree with them.

Michael was tall and rangy, with broad shoulders stretching his uniform taut, dwarfing the small, voluptuous figure in his arms. He was not handsome in the conventional manner, he was too rugged looking, but he was a strong-looking man, with a crew-cut (according to regulations), black hair and deep blue eyes. He exuded masculinity. She though dreamily as she looked up at him that he looked just like Gary Cooper, if Gary Cooper had talked more and had a crew cut. She found Michael even more exciting.

He was tapped on the shoulder again. He half-turned, exasperated, and then, recognizing the short, stocky sailor next to him, said with relief, "Oh, Pete! What's going on?" Pete took a good look at the young woman beside him and continued to gaze at her breasts, insolently, while he responded to Michael. Ruth squirmed inwardly, but she steadfastly maintained a calm demeanor, not wanting to antagonize a friend of Michael's, but wishing he would leave them alone.

"The guys are getting up a party, Mike. Come on—it'll be fun."

"I don't know," Michael hesitated, also looking down at Ruth.

"It'll be fun, Mike, really fun," and Pete emphasized his words with a meaningful look. "Why do you want to stay in this dump? Maybe the broad would like to come with us."

"Well . . ." and Michael looked again at Ruth. "Would you like to go?"

Ruth knew she couldn't. Her heart seemed to pound so loud that all she could hear in her ears was its roar. She wanted to, but found herself saying, "I just can't, Michael, I can't. Could you—could you," and she lifted her face boldly and looked at him. Asking a boy to stay with her was not in her code of ethics. She cleared her throat, which seemed blocked. "Could you please stay? I would like you to stay." She whispered the last shamefacedly.

He seemed undecided. "Give me a minute, Pete," he said and he swung her away to a corner of the room. His voice deepened. "Let me take you home?" he whispered in her ear.

"Yes," she replied, smiling up at him. The smile was full of promise, but she knew not what she promised. She was innocence garbed in provocative sophistication. She only knew that she like Michael and that she was attracted to him. And, she loved to neck.

The sweet strains of Glen Miller's "Moonlight Serenade" swung to a stop, and they parted and faced each other once again, studying the other's face. "Okay!" Michael exclaimed, and his voice spoke volumes. "Let's go. Oh hell, excuse me, Ruth, I've got to go tell Pete—and my mother."

"Your mother?" She couldn't believe what she was hearing. This was wartime. All of these restless, swarming boys (she couldn't think of them as men) came from everywhere else in the country, not from the San Francisco Bay area. "Did you say your mother?"

"Yes," and he grinned a bit sheepishly. "She's a Senior Hostess here. I'm home on leave, and she talked me into coming tonight. Come on, I'll introduce you."

Ruth intuitively did not want to go with him to see his mother. He pulled her gently off the dance floor. He laughed. "But I guess you know her already, don't you? Mrs. Stratton . . ."

Fortunately, they had just reached Pete, and Michael didn't see her pained expression.

"Hey, Pete. Sorry buddy, I'm not going with you. But I'll see you later, okay?"

She tugged on his sleeve. "I have to get my coat, Michael, and make an excuse to leave early. We can't be seen leaving with the servicemen. And I want to tell my girlfriend that I'm leaving." Whenever either Ruth or Sally met a likely prospect, she allowed him to take her home while the other young woman went home alone, perfectly safe on the streets of San Francisco at night in the year 1942.

"Sure, if that's what you want," he told her. "See you later, alligator."

Michael was exuberant. He congratulated himself that he had let Pete talk him into stopping in at the Pro Station to pick up a few of the foil-wrapped condoms, neatly attached to each other, before they went on leave. He suspected Pete knew he was a virgin, a fact he was heartily ashamed of and wished to rectify as soon as possible. His wallet, thanks to Pete, was now well stocked. Pete really looked after him, maybe because they were both San Francisco boys, although they had grown up in vastly different circumstances. Pete Roffola, the third of seven children, was tough because he had to be tough to survive in Butchertown, where the slaughterhouses were, over by Third Street. Michael Stratton was the only child of a wealthy widow in the prestigious Seacliff district.

Ruth responded automatically to Michael in the standard manner. "In a while, crocodile," and she turned and made her way to the cloakroom.

CHAPTER 3

Would you like to come in for a cup of Postum?" She looked down, her house key in hand, unable to meet the brightness of his eyes. The practically-new powder bluc 1940 Chrysler Highlander he drove had impressed her no less than it had the first time she rode in it last night. He had seemed a little disappointed when she hadn't asked him in at the time, although of course they had made a later date for the Japanese Tea Garden. The convertible must be his father's, she guessed. She was more used to riding streetcars. The sailors she met in the Port of San Francisco usually did not have an automobile at their beck and call.

He nodded happily. Hearing nothing, she then looked up. He nodded again, in mock gravity and they both laughed.

He asked, a bit puzzled, "Postum? Not coffee?" And then he knew the answer. "Say, Ruth, I'm sorry. That's rationed too, isn't it?"

She threw him a quick glance. "You don't mind?" He shook his head, his eyes caressing her. She led the way into the kitchen, whispering matter-of-factly, "You boys need it more than we do. I have two brothers in the service, you know."

He whispered back, automatically. "Oh yes, I saw the two stars on the flag in the window. Where are they stationed?" Then—"Why are we whispering?"

"My folks go to bed early." He followed her practically on tiptoe, with no wish to wake her parents. The faint sounds of her father's snoring reassured them both.

A shadow came into her eyes as she answered his question, even while she busied herself boiling the water for their Postum. "Harry is in the South Pacific, and Jerry is a bomber pilot in England. David is married. He and Debbie have two darling baby girls—Lisa is a year old, and Susan is three—so he hasn't been drafted yet."

Michael scanned the room as she took out two of the pretty cups and saucers that her parents had picked up free at the movies on "China Night." The kitchen was clean and cheerful, with frilly yellow curtains on the one window and a matching yellow patterned oilcloth on the kitchen table.

"Gee, I'm sorry, we have no cake. How about toast and jam? We have raisin toast." She seemed stricken because of the bareness of the cupboard.
"Sure, that would be great," he replied.

She chattered away nervously. "Of course, I have no butter to put on the bread. Just this horrible margarine. I mix up that white stuff with the yellow powder myself, but I can't seem to get a good buttery color. It comes out with yellow streaks, as usual. Very unappetizing, I'm afraid . . ." Privately, she felt sure that the "white stuff" was plain lard, but that was better left unsaid.

Michael was reminded again of the differences in available food between the Armed Forces (especially the Navy) and the civilian population. Butter was plentiful on the tables in the mess hall.

She hesitated again. "It tastes so horrible. Would you want just the toast and jam? It isn't so bad that way." With the ration points at sixteen for butter and only four for the margarine, there really wasn't much choice for civilians, but she was embarrassed and humiliated nonetheless.

He felt an unaccustomed tenderness for Ruth, obviously trying her best to please, and so handicapped in her efforts. "That's the way I always eat it," he lied. "Much better that way."

They sipped the Postum, which he really didn't care for, although Ruth seemed to savor it, and nibbled at the toast and jam. After a somewhat too hearty, "Say, this is great," he subsided into silence.

She nervously tried another line of conversation. "I've know your mother for a long time at the USO," she blurted out. And then, horrified, she realized that was definitely not what she wanted to say.

He perked up at this. "Yes, Mom likes the volunteer work. Makes her feel as if she's doing her part for the war effort, you know."

"A very nice lady." Ruth couldn't look him in the eye.

"Thanks. I think so." He sounded no more sincere than Ruth and the conversation once again lagged.

"I'm a virgin, you know," she said, apropos of nothing. *That should keep the evening under control*, she thought.

He almost choked on his raisin toast. "Are you alright?" she asked innocently, enjoying herself. His choking sputtered to a stop. He drank a bit more of the Postum to gain time to think.

"Sorry," he replied a bit cautiously, no longer certain of what awaited him. "That's very interesting." He was desperate to change the subject. "Say, what do you think of Glenn Miller? Isn't he absolutely great? I think he's the best around."

"Oh yes, I just love him." She really didn't have an opinion, but she wanted to please him. "Much better than Harry James or Cab Calloway." She felt herself floundering again.

"Well, I do like Harry James, too. That trumpet just can't be beat. And Cab Calloway's "Heidi-hi Heidi-ho" is really pretty jazzy, you know? But you're right about Miller—he's the best."

"Were you born here?" she asked. She still couldn't get over the novelty of meeting a sailor from her hometown.

"Oh yes, we've lived at Seacliff forever. My grandparents built the house years ago."

She was startled. Seacliff was the most expensive district in town. He was obviously from old money. His socialite mother was worlds apart from her Jewish immigrant parents. The thought made her more nervous than ever.

"What about you?"

"My mother and father came from Germany when they were first married. My mother was pregnant, and she wanted to have the baby in America."

"Was that you?"

"Oh no, that was my oldest brother, David. I'm the youngest."

"I'll bet your parents were really glad when you came along," he said warmly.

"Yes, they had always wanted a girl." She didn't mention the difficult years of illness and restriction she'd gone through.

"I'm an only child. My father died when I was three—I really don't remember him. There's just me and my mother in San Francisco, although back East I have uncles, aunts, cousins—you know," he laughed softly. "Just one big happy family."

"We only have each other," she responded simply. "No other relatives that we know of. I do love the City, though. The Japanese Tea Garden is my very favorite place—in spite of everything, of course." She couldn't help giggling again.

"Yes, it's great—especially with everything," he grinned. "I like Fleischaker's Pool, too. Good for a really refreshing swim in that salt water."

She didn't want to disagree with him, but she was beginning to feel a little more secure. "I like it, but I don't like the idea of the tiny fishes and fish eggs coming through that pipe. Come to think of it, I guess a swimmer in the sea would meet even bigger fish."

"And even bigger fish eggs!" And they both laughed.

"You could always eat them, you know," he said in mock seriousness. "Caviar under water!"

They had nothing in common, really, but laughter. And that was all they needed. They talked and then they kissed, and the chemistry was strong between them. They left the kitchen and wandered into the front room, and Ruth forgot about his mother and her nervousness. She was in an enchanted world, and naught but good could enter there.

He, too seemed deeply drawn to Ruth—and for the first time in a long time it wasn't just chemistry. He genuinely liked her.

They necked blissfully, the electric sparks flying, both carefully measuring how far it was safe to go. The fact that they both knew limits were imposed added even more fuel to their mutual desire. He tentatively and experimentally tried to go a little further than she was willing to allow him and was surprised to feel relieved, in spite of his frustration, when she stopped him, breathless from her own intensity.

He leaned back against the sofa and smiled at her, pulling out a rumpled pack of cigarettes and offering her one.

"No thanks, I don't smoke." She smiled back. She noticed the brand name on the pack. "Would you walk a mile for a Camel?" she asked playfully, quoting the well-known slogan, as he lighted up.

"No, honey, not unless I was lost in the desert. But I sure would walk a mile for you—anywhere." He put his arm around her and they laughed together again.

"Is it true that Lucky Strike really did make a cigarette just for the armed forces?" She felt so comfortable cozied up next to him.

"Well, not exactly. 'Lucky Strike has gone to war' just means that they changed the package color from green to white when the war started, and now it's white for us and white for you," and he began laughing again.

She joined him. "I know what you're laughing at."

He looked at her, still chuckling. "No, you don't." This girl was too innocent to have heard the new parody of L-S-M-F-T, which was supposed to stand for "Lucky Strike Means Fine Tobacco." He felt very protective towards her.

But Ruth wanted to show how worldly and sophisticated she was. "Oh, yes I do!" A girlfriend had told her. "It's L-S-M-F-T," and she collapsed into giggles. She found she couldn't actually say the words after all.

They both left it at that, the unspoken bond between them—"Let's Screw, My Finger's Tired"—seemed too naughty to be spoken aloud, but both were still laughing when he left shortly afterwards, with her telephone number safely in his pocket.

CHAPTER 4

"Ruth Braunstein!" Mary Stratton was deeply shocked. "You saw Ruth Braunstein? Did that hussy take you home to her house from the USO?"

Too late, Michael remembered the USO rules. "Not really, Mother. I happened to—uhh—run into her outside."

Mrs. Stratton knew very well the custom of meeting the boys in front of the corner restaurant, and she had even suggested to one or two of the very shy young ladies (not like Ruth Braunstein) herself that, although she, of course, couldn't advocate it, it had been known to be possible. And didn't Michael come to her Saturday night full of high spirits and say he was leaving early and taking the car? And she had to take a taxi home! For Ruth Braunstein? She bit her lips at the thought that she herself had actually talked him into attending the USO dance. She had thought he might meet a nice girl, one with a family, not a—

"That young lady is not your type, Michael. She's just not our class, dear." She controlled any stronger language that she was tempted to employ.

"Type? Class? This is 1942, Mother, and we're a world at war. If you would have seen what I have, you wouldn't speak of type and class." Actually, Michael had never seen real combat. What he had seen was limited to what was to be seen at boot camp in San Diego, California, along with a brief stay at the Corpus Christi Naval Air Station in Texas, where he had been exposed to some unnerving examples of deep poverty for the first time in his life. He had read a great deal, however, and Ernie Pyle's description of the front line was terrifyingly real. Even something as old as All Quiet on the Western Front by that German writer, told from his side's viewpoint, was frightening. *Strange that we were fighting the Germans again.*

He shook his head, as if the memories were too horrible to contemplate, and looked again at his mother. She did seem unduly disturbed. What did she have against Ruth, anyway? Her next words cleared up the mystery.

"Ruth is probably very nice, dear," and her tone belied the statement, thought she was choosing her words carefully now, "but she is a bit fast, you know. I have reason to believe that she might be promiscuous." And then, in a too-casual manner, she said: "You do know that she's Jewish, don't you dear?"

"Oh, Mother!" He looked at her helplessly. "I have reason to believe that she is a very nice girl, even though her family isn't too well off and she is Jewish. After all, Mother, I'm not going to marry the girl! I'm just going to date her for a bit."

"Well, all right then," and Mrs. Stratton left the study, where they had been having the discussion, since the maid had entered to dust, and she certainly didn't want Miss Big Ears to hear this. She was satisfied. Boys must sow their wild oats, and apparently that was all that this was. Ruth was so—so common. She shuddered delicately. She could have asked for someone a bit more acceptable, but for wild oats she couldn't be too selective.

Mary Stratton was a tall, aristocratic-looking woman in her early forties, the type that was called "tweedy," only partially because of her excellent quality casual clothes. She was slender to the point of being too thin, with a flat bosom as well as flat shoes. Her hair was prematurely white, and her coiffeur was faultless, with never a hair out of place. She was once a beautiful woman, but she had not aged well, and her cold pale blue eyes and thin lips made her truly formidable.

Mary Stratton had a deep dislike and distrust of sensuality. That part of her married life had been very distasteful to her, as she was certain that it would have been to any real lady, and she had been relieved when she became pregnant so soon after the wedding so that she wouldn't have to tolerate that animal behavior for at least nine months. Afterwards, when Edward was in that terrible auto accident when Michael was only three, she mourned for her husband, of course, but at least she didn't have to subject herself to that again. She realized, though, that men had those needs, and she was resigned to it in her only son.

Michael, left alone in the room with Bridget, the maid, was thoughtful. His Mother had not been in favor of any of the young society girls he had dated in his high school years, never seeming to like any of them, but she had never been so vehement in her disapproval before. This even surpassed the anger she had expressed when he had volunteered for the Navy right after high school. He was barely eighteen, and of course she wanted him to go to college, where she could have probably arranged for a commission for him, but he didn't want to wait. His buddies were all going in, and he wasn't going to miss one minute of it. With maturity (and his recent reading of Ernie Pyle), he did wonder if perhaps what he might have missed might have been destruction, but the camaraderie he found in the Navy, even among sailors of the so-called "lower class," he thought sardonically, was fast becoming most important in his life. Ruth Braunstein was only a girl he liked and who liked him, that was all. He repressed his memory of the strong physical attraction between them. And he knew she wasn't fast, regardless of what his mother said. The thought occurred to him that his mother might actually be jealous, but he dismissed that as preposterous.

He looked at Bridget affectionately. He had known her all his life. She was a tough, resilient Irishwoman with flyaway brownish hair, a lived-in face, and warm, lively brown eyes. She had "come over from the Ould Countly when I was a slip of a lass," to hear her tell it. Her brogue had softened during the years so that it was hardly noticeable, but nothing else had softened in Bridget.

She continued dusting vigorously, glancing at the young man. "Michael? A tiff with the old lady, is it?" Mary Stratton had never been able to impress upon her the importance of calling the young master of the family, "Mr. Michael," which Bridget Flaherty thought ridiculous, since she was the main diaperer and bottle washer of the baby Michael—and his confidante through the years. Mrs. Stratton didn't know she was referred to as "the old lady." Michael and Bridget understood each other completely.

"Nothing, really," he replied, grinning at the older women. Her uniform swished back and forth on her square body as she wielded the large feather duster as if it were a weapon. She looked at him knowingly. He cleared his throat. "Just a new girlfriend, old girl, that Mother is less than happy about."

"Hmph! And since when has she ever been happy with one? And that Lucille such a sweet lass, too. I've always told you, boyo—follow your heart.

I didn't, and look where I ended up!" And she gave a particularly vicious thrust with the duster. They both knew that she had really followed her heart, for her heart lay with Michael and not with her gentleman friend (whom Michael suspected was imaginary) of long ago.

"I just don't know what you'd do without me, Michael. 'Tis due to me, me lad, that you turned out to be such a fine, upstanding young man. Purely due to me!" She finished the dusting with a flourish. "Remember, follow your—" and she swallowed the rest as footsteps neared the door.

"Bridget!" Mrs. Stratton called. Please see to the kitchen. I want you to give Cook that good recipe of yours for Beef Wellington."

"Yes, Ma'am." Bridget turned. "I've finished here anyway." Now to do battle with Cook, who resented fiercely any forays into her domain, particularly when they consisted of telling her how to cook. Bridget sighed.

CHAPTER 5

"So you had a phone call. Didn't I tell you?" Etta Braunstein attempted to look confused and failed.

"No Mama, you did not. Who was it and when did he call?" Ruth was on her way to being angry, but not quite there.

"So I'm telling you now. So you know it was a 'he,' do you?"

"Mama!" Ruth's voice rose, and Etta hurriedly told her what she wanted to hear.

"It was the boy you went to the Japanese Tea Garden with—Michael. He called about 3:00 this afternoon. I told him you worked for a living and you'd be home later. So I'm not such a bad message-taker after all, am I?"

"Oh, Michael. His name's Michael Stratton, Mama." Ruth's voice and mood had softened considerably.

"Michael Stratton!" Etta Braunstein shook her head. "He's not Jewish? He's a goy?"

"So what's wrong with that? He's very nice, and I like him," Ruth retorted defensively.

"So what's wrong with a nice Jewish boy?" Her mother responded, answering a question with question as usual, her slight Yiddish accent exaggerated as if to demonstrate the difference.

"Oh, it's not serious," Ruth lied, flouncing away. "I do like him, though."

But it was serious with Ruth. She had thought of nothing else but Michael since he left. She had stayed awake for ages, savoring over and over every moment of the weekend she had spent with him; and, when she finally fell asleep, she dreamed of him—but it was a disturbing dream. He was on a hill, at the very top, and she was struggling up to him through rocks and thorny bushes, which tore her clothes and hurt her. He just stood there, watching her struggle, and then he disappeared; and a witch with a long black conical hat, who looked remarkably like Margaret Hamilton, the wicked witch in the movie The Wizard of Oz, took his place. When Ruth stopped in horror, the hill disappeared, and Michael and she were together in a pretty little house with a white picket fence and having Postum together. Then they were in bed together—and she woke up. She always seemed to wake up before she really made love in any of her dreams, perhaps because she didn't know exactly how to orchestrate it.

Ruth knew all the arguments against dating Gentile boys. She had heard them often enough. Besides, she knew firsthand the deeply penetrating and bewildering hurt she felt when an acquaintance or, worse, a friend offhandedly and casually made a remark or a joke about the Jews. It didn't even have to be derogatory (though it usually was), it still hurt. She knew she was ultrasensitive about it, but generations of anti-Semitism had prepared the way.

One didn't run into that when one dated only Jewish boys. Her mother's logic, too, that with the same culture, the same background, the same interests, two people had more of a chance at happiness—was an uncontestable argument.

All the sensible rationalizations came to naught beside the simple fact that Ruth was very rapidly falling in love with a man she had just met. Part of it was falling in love with love, part was chemistry, and the most important part was finding a friend she could talk to, feel comfortable with, and have fun with.

Etta Braunstein was concerned as she did the dinner dishes. She was perceptive enough to realize that Ruth was infatuated with the glamour of the young man, and what she had heard from Ruth about him (and his mother) filled her with a sense of foreboding. The main thing was the happiness of Ruth, her only daughter, her baby. That was all that really mattered. She wanted a good life for her so badly that it hurt. Also, there had never been a mixed marriage in her family or in Max's family, thank God, and this was no time to start. Max would never stand for it. They wanted a grandson bar mitzvah'd, not a child brought up as a Gentile! She wouldn't change David's adorable baby girls for the world, but a boy would be nice too. Her pepper and salt hair waved gently about her worried plump face, and her large brown eyes were more soulful than usual. Only the humor in those eyes and the laugh lines about her generous mouth, which was noted for its outspoken-ness, saved her from being plain. Her multi-colored flowered housedress was stretched alarmingly over her broad hips and, unfortunately, made her look even more overweight than she was. She wore flat slippers with lisle stockings, as she always did in the house, because she had trouble with her feet. When she went out, she put on sensible shoes with low heels.

Etta and Ruth got along fairly well—as well as two strong women in one family ever do. They loved each other, but each had their own very definite ideas about practically everything, so they argued frequently. Sometimes the arguments themselves were a form of love.

Etta smiled as she recalled a friend of Ruth's who had come to dinner one night before the boys went to war. David was married already to Debbie, and they had little Susan had been born in that tiny apartment in the Mission District. Ruth's guest was a young Gentile girl of English parentage (Etta couldn't recall her name at the moment). She was so frightened at the arguments that went on at the dinner table, with the two boys, Harry and Jerry, their little sister Ruth, Etta, and Max seemingly all talking at once at the top their lungs, that Etta had kindly stopped the noisy conversation in mid-syllable and explained to the young girl that no one was angry, that they were just having a discussion, and that they were all enjoying themselves. The youngster, however, was not convinced and left shortly thereafter, still frightened.

Etta heard the telephone ring over the rush of the water for the dishes and knew instinctively who it was. She quietly turned off the faucet and unashamedly listened to her daughter's conversation.

"Hello. Oh, hi." Ruth's voice became warm and seductive. Etta shook her head. Didn't she have enough worries with two of her boys at war? How was she going to keep this one a virgin until she was safely married? Then, no matter how she listened (and she had good ears), she couldn't hear a thing. Ruth had taken the phone away from the hall on its long cord, brought it into her room, and closed the door. Etta, still shaking her head, went back to her dishes.

Michael was also taking precautions as to privacy. He had waited until his mother was out of the house, attending a lecture by some flower arranger or other—he had pleaded a headache plus non-interest in the subject, which was exactly half true—before he ventured to pick up the extension phone in the study. "Hello. How are you doing?"

"Fine, Michael. And you?"

"Great. Say—I'm sorry I missed you this afternoon."

"Oh, I guess I forgot to tell you—I work at The White House. I'm a salesgirl there."

"That's nice." He cleared his throat. "Are you busy tonight, Ruth?"

"No." Her tone was in invitation.

"I was just wondering if you'd like to go to a movie tonight. The Fox has John Garfield in Air Force—if you're interested."

"The Fox! Oh, yes, Michael, I love to go there." She was more interested in the theater, which she had attended too few times, than the movie. The Fox, at the corner of Tenth and Market Streets, was a movie palace that outshone some royal palaces. "What a perfectly wonderful idea—and how nice of you to think of it," Ruth purred.

Her warm sincerity came through the telephone, and Michael warmed in response. "I've always enjoyed it, too." Then his voice deepened. "I've missed you."

"I've missed you, too," she whispered, and the two young people sat by the phone in blissful silence, too full of feeling to speak.

He recovered first. "I'll pick you up in an hour. O.K.?"

"Fine." She would have to rush to be ready in time, but she could make it. They rang off, and she ran to her mother.

"Mama, Michael's coming over. We're going to the Fox to see a movie with John Garfield—Air Force, I think—and he'll be here in an hour." She stopped chattering and looked closely at her mother. She hesitated, unwilling to hurt her feelings. "Mama, you know that nice black dress you got last year?"

"No." Her mother turned and glared at her. "He will see me as I am. What's the matter—you don't like your old mama the way she is?"

"No, no, Mama." She tried to cover up. "I just want everything nice for him," she ended lamely.

"So." Etta Braunstein turned back to the sink. It had been a simple pot roast dinner, but it did seem as if every dish in the kitchen had been used. For only three people yet! She never asked for help as long as she was able, please God, but sometimes an offer would be welcome. "So a Jewish girl and a Gentile boy, after going to the Japanese Tea Garden, are going to the show. And after? Some Chinese food maybe?"

Ruth laughed and then thought. "You know, that would be fun. Who knows? I don't know if he likes Chinese food," and she ran off to get ready.

"At least I won't have to wash the dishes from the Chinese food," Mrs. Braunstein called after her meaningfully. "All by myself!" in a louder tone, in case her daughter missed the hint.

"Oh, Mama, I would have helped if I would have thought—but I have to run now. Why didn't you ask me?"

"So why didn't you offer?" Now that Ruth was feeling properly guilty, Mrs. Braunstein was satisfied for the moment. "Go run along. Have a good time and enjoy."

Ruth ran back, kissed her mother in love and understanding, and ran out of the kitchen again.

CHAPTER 6

They didn't finish that date with Chinese food. They drove to Ocean Beach, where they walked and talked in the sand, Ruth carrying her shoes. They ordered enchiladas at one of the little restaurants that lined the beach, and nothing had ever tasted so good to them.They discussed the opulence of the Fox Theatre, from the Napoleonic vases that adorned the mezzanine to the gold and crystal chandeliers and plush red carpet, to the special cosmetic stands in the ladies' lounge and the library in the men's lounge. The huge Wurlitzer organ in the orchestra pit stood majestically in front of the most beautiful drapes Ruth had ever seen, seemingly woven of gold and jewels, and there were two other organs, one on the stage and the third in the lobby to entertain anyone who happened to be waiting for seats. Michael had one criticism of the movie, however. When John Garfield, as Gunner Winocki, grabbed a .50-caliber machine gun to successfully hip-shoot a Japanese Zero down, Michael actually laughed, in spite of the suspense involved. He informed Ruth that, in reality, the gun's recoil would have knocked John Garfield flatter than the Zero. They ended the day perfectly, with tender and loving caresses, which never, however, went too far.

They had many dates after that, and both families became alarmed in their own way. Max Braunstein was all for forbidding Ruth to ever see Michael again, but Etta talked him out of that. As she wisely pointed out, that would only make her more determined to see him, and wouldn't they rather have her seeing the young man openly instead of sneaking around? Etta used her questions for more than answering questions. Etta thought if the entire matter could run its course, wouldn't it collapse when Michael's leave ended and he had to go away, just like her other boyfriends? Wouldn't it be best to just leave them alone—not alone in the house, she hastened to add—no sense asking for trouble—but not to show their disapproval of the young man?

Their disapproval was there, however, in the very air, and Ruth, even more perceptive than her mother, felt it strongly.

On the other side of the tracks, Mrs. Stratton was mildly appalled. Even though she still labored under the delusion that Ruth was the recipient of Michael's "wild oats," it was going on far too long to suit her. That little tramp is actually trying to ensnare him, she thought to herself. How very insolent. She noted that Ruth hadn't attended on her usual Saturday night at the USO. And Michael was gone on Saturday and Sunday, night and day, as well as on both Wednesday and Friday nights since he met her. His entire two-week leave seemed devoted to that woman. She had confronted him, asking him if he were seeing Ruth, and the answer was, "Of course. She's a very nice girl, Mother," in a tone one might use to a slightly backward child. She ignored it, of course. Well, he would leave in another week; and, though she would be sorry to see him go, he would be beyond the reach of that creature.

She was not an angry woman. She didn't have any strong emotions at all, and she didn't understand or feel comfortable with those who did. Sometimes she suspected that Michael was over-emotional, but he seemed to control himself sufficiently when he was with her. She was annoyed, however.

Michael wasn't home long enough to feel any disapproval. He had long since armored himself against his mother. He kept himself busy during the day buddying with Pete at Lefty O'Doul's or one of the other bars, dropping into an afternoon movie, or looking up his old friends, most who were on active duty themselves. He always enjoyed Pete; he loved the movies; and he was delighted to find George Simpson a 4-F. George, 250 pounds of solid muscle, had been a guard on the high school football team and had bragged endlessly about what he was going to do to the Japs when he got around to it. George, however, discovered he had flat feet and was rejected by the military.

Michael's nights were for Ruth—that is, on Wednesdays and Fridays, and on the weekends, of course. She insisted upon going to sleep early the rest of the week for some reason. Apparently she needed more sleep than the average person. He knew she got up fairly early in the morning to report to The White House for her job, but he could stay up until 2:00 a.m. and still awaken at 6:30 in the morning feeling fresh. And he loved being with her. Perhaps he was even falling in love with her.

It was their last night together, the night before Michael's leave ended, that Ruth told him of her childhood, of the rheumatic fever that darkened those years, of the doctors that told her parents that she could never live to adulthood, that she could never have a normal life. "But I can, I can!" She looked up at him appealingly, with the tears streaming down her fact. "I know I can. After all, I've reached adulthood, haven't I? I'm eighteen years old—draft age, if I were a man. Sometimes I do get tired, but if I get enough rest I'm all right again." She paused for a moment to gain control of herself. "Does it—does it make a difference?" She whispered the last so that he had to bend down to hear her.

"No, of course not," he responded automatically, not knowing if it were the truth or not. He was really shaken to think that perhaps Ruth "couldn't lead a normal life." Did that mean no sex? No children? But the doctors were wrong about her growing up. Maybe they were wrong about this, too. But what if they weren't?

She realized his shock and, with unwanted tears still choking her, managed to utter the most difficult sentence she had ever spoken. "Michael—Michael, I—I will understand if you don't want to see me again," and she turned away, hating her uncontrollable tears, trying to hide her face from him.

There was a short silence, and Ruth's heart sank. She kept her head down, afraid to look up at Michael. Did she really mean so little to him? But maybe she was asking too much.

Michael was shocked and unsure. He wasn't ready to give her up, either. "Of course I want to see you again, Ruth," and though the words were true, they had a hollow sound. He attempted to laugh. "Everything's copasetic. Don't worry, honey."

She swallowed bravely. Perhaps she had lost him. It was the first time she had encountered heartbreak. It really <u>did</u> feel that something was breaking inside. Well, she had done all she could. If she had lost him—well, she'd manage somehow. What else could she do? And she couldn't envision any future without him.

They parted early that night. There didn't seem much to talk about. They kissed goodbye, and Michael said he would write, and Ruth murmured that she would, too.

As he left, going down the steps, she whispered, "God go with you and keep you safe, Michael," and he, startled, turned to her again. He slowly retraced his steps back to the small figure waiting at the front door. "Take care, sweetheart," he said softly, as he held her to him for one last time, and he was gone.

And Ruth wondered if she would ever see him again.

CHAPTER 7

It was an interminably long year from 1942 to 1943. Ruth read the growing report of fatalities with increasing fear. That nice Mrs. Olson, the white-haired cashier at the store, lost her only son, and the flag in front of the Olson home now bore a gold star instead of a blue one. When Mrs. Olson came back to work after only one day to grieve, Ruth, with deep empathy, wondered why she didn't take more time off. Once, as Mrs. Olson worked steadily, her eyes desperate, but her mouth firm, Ruth ventured to put her hand on the older woman's arm in mute sympathy. The lady nodded and even managed a sad little smile, "Work, helps, dear." And then Ruth, her own eyes filling with the tears Mrs. Olson refused to allow, understood.

Ruth was young, however, and despite the fact that she missed Michael terribly, she still wanted to enjoy herself, which, fortunately, did not at all conflict with what she perceived as her patriotic duty to entertain servicemen. She tried to continue to attend the USO dances on her usual Saturday nights with Sally, but Mrs. Stratton singled Ruth out by treating her as if she weren't there, even when she ventured a timid "Hello" as she went by. Although Michael's mother smiled at Sally pleasantly, she managed to convey ice-cold hostility and contempt to Ruth. After three such rebuffs, Ruth resolutely tried to avoid her, but it was almost impossible, and the strain showed clearly on her expressive, miserable face. Only one very small and thin sailor, clad in his summer white uniform, which was rare in San Francisco even on a hot and sticky night like this one, asked her to dance. Since her precious nylons had run long ago, Ruth had painted on her usual brown leg makeup. She hadn't noticed that the leg paint was softening and running a bit, but, when they parted after the dance, she did notice, appalled, that her partner had brown stains on one of his trouser legs. He followed her glance and turned bright red, believing it had somehow happened earlier. They permanently parted by mutual consent. He was bewildered and embarrassed, and she was fervently hoping he wouldn't find out exactly how it had happened.

She saw that Sally seemed to be having a good time, dancing and laughing up at an almost too-handsome soldier who responded eagerly, so Ruth tried to stick it out. When she finally managed to get Sally alone, however, she told her she wanted to leave because she felt so badly, and it was not a lie. Her head ached, and her stomach was in turmoil. Sally knew all about Mrs. Stratton, of course, and sympathized with Ruth, but she wanted to know the soldier a bit better, so she stayed, planning to let him escort her home, while Ruth left alone.

When Ruth let herself into the house, after an unusually long wait transferring between the two streetcars she had to take, she went right into her room. She took out her all too small treasure trove of V-mail letters from Michael to read and re-read again. This was the only part of her life Ruth didn't share with Sally. She would tell Sally when she heard from Michael (and sometimes complained that he didn't write often enough), but his words were for her alone. She herself wrote him every week.

She poured over the letters, trying to read between the lines, holding them secretly to herself.

The letters were a comfort, but she cried herself to sleep.

Understandably, Ruth no longer wished to attend the USO dances. When she suggested to Sally that they go to the Hospitality House for servicemen ("Hop House" to them) instead, the taller girl was amenable to trying it out, but she didn't want to give up the USO completely. So Sally agreeably changed her night at the USO to Friday night, where she enjoyed herself alone, but the two of them then attended the Hop House on Saturday nights. It wasn't as structured or restrictive as the USO, but Ruth met her dates there. She didn't know why—perhaps because the war had been going on so long—but the boys now seemed wilder, less controllable. The more dates she went out on, the more she appreciated Michael. Al from Alabama was one of her bad experiences.

When she met the tall, blonde, good-looking Southern boy at the Hop House, he seemed nice enough, though not too bright. She allowed him to take her home and dated him a few times, more for the companionship than for any real attraction. One night, after an early movie, she invited him in for Postum. She was surprised to find that her parents had gone out for the evening to her brother's apartment and had not returned as yet.

Al wouldn't sit still long enough to drink the Postum. Although he hadn't seemed aggressive on their previous dates, now all he wanted to do was neck—and more. He tried again and again to break down her defenses as she tried to limit him to kisses, under the misapprehension that the kisses would satisfy him. When that only seemed to inflame him further, she used the defense that had never failed her, that of telling him she was a virgin. Instead of dousing his raging ardor, however, it seemed to raise him to new heights. She realized almost immediately that somehow, inexplicably, this was the wrong statement to make to Al, and that she had made a terrible mistake.

He was a muscular, strong young man, and Ruth began to panic. "Don't worry, honey," he gasped between grabs. "I want to marry you."

"Marry me!" She was shocked. "You just met me! Besides," and she desperately continued to push aside his groping hands, "I—do—not—want—to—marry you!" Her words were punctuated with the effort she was making—but she was losing. He actually stopped at that point and looked at her strangely. She sat back, relieved that he had a last stopped. "Honey, don't you understand? Just relax and enjoy it. Then you'll have to marry me." He finished that amazingly simple statement with a self-righteous air and redoubled his efforts.

Not knowing what else to do, she got off the sofa, where he had practically pushed her, and they actually began the classical chase in rather slow motion, all around the furniture from room to room, although Ruth specifically avoided the bedrooms. She was in deadly fear her parents would return and forbid her ever to go out again, and she was frantically hoping that they would come home and stop this idiot.

She was too keyed up to cry, too frightened to do anything but try to keep sufficient space between them, but he caught her between the kitchen table and the stove. There was nothing else to do. Desperate, she put her hands over her face and pretended to cry. Al changed immediately. He seemed to think that she had been pretending before, but that her tears (crocodile though they were) proved she was sincere. He began looking for his hat, which had been squashed into the sofa during one of their tussles, and she began breathing again.

Ruth was bewildered and frightened. Now that it was over and he was really leaving, she was filled with thankfulness that, not only had she escaped this maniac, but her parents hadn't walked in on them in the middle of that stupid chase. She felt as if she were in a silly movie with the Marx Brothers, where Harpo was chasing her around the house—except that that this was real and wasn't funny.

Before Al left, however, he actually turned around and asked her, in a perfectly pleasant tone, when he could see her again. Her indignation at this innocent question was greater than the fear she still felt. "No! Absolutely not! I do not wish to see you again." She spit the words out between her teeth.

Al seemed to be mildly surprised. His large blue eyes blinked once or twice, and he murmured, "All right, then," as he went down the steps.

Ruth bounced back quickly. The next week she was at the Hop House as usual, but she decided never to volunteer the information about her virginity again.

With John it was different. There she was ashamed of herself. When he asked her to dance at the Hop House, she was hesitant. He was in mismatched, ill-fitting civilian clothes, a less than honorable uniform for a healthy young man at the time. He had the look of a clean-shaven young hobo. She slowly accompanied him to dance, privately wondering how he ever was permitted into the Hop House, which was supposed to be only for servicemen. Their first few moments on the dance floor were silent, awkward. Then his words tumbled over themselves in his eagerness to tell her, without her asking, that he was a Merchant Marine, that he had had his ship sunk under him, and that he was in whatever clothes could be found. After that he was silent again. Ruth was filled with swift compassion and sympathy, but she couldn't find the proper words to express herself. She had to content herself with bright, inconsequential remarks, which he answered in monosyllables.

When he, with obvious difficulty, got up his courage to ask to take her home, she didn't have the heart to refuse, though she felt completely inadequate to supply the psychiatric help he clearly needed. Her experience with Al had left her with the conviction that Al was not completely sane, and this man really had an excuse for instability. It was plainly an effort for him to talk at all, and she accepted immediately, hoping the fear she felt did not show.

She ventured a real question as they walked out. "When did your ship sink, John?" thinking perhaps it would be best for him to talk about it, but not really knowing if it were the right thing to do or not. She decided to go with her instincts and see if she could help him by sympathetically listening to him.

"I don't remember exactly," he hesitantly answered, after a moment, "But they told me to come straight here, to relax, after I got the clothes." He looked at her helplessly. "I'm so sorry about the clothes."

"Oh, don't worry about that," she lied brightly. "I don't even think about that!" She was already ashamed of herself for even considering his appearance, which was certainly no fault of his. He was actually a hero, she kept telling herself as they emerged from the Hop House into the usual crowd of late-nighters coming and going around Market Street. The hostile glares he was getting included her, just for being with him. It hadn't been so bad inside the Hop House, where apparently the other servicemen and the senior hostesses understood, but he couldn't very well wear a sign outside announcing his war-casualty status.

She couldn't seem to help herself. Even while telling herself continually that he was a war hero, she found herself walking further and further apart from him until they were almost on opposite sides of the broad sidewalk. Perhaps no one would know she was with him. People walked between them. He stared straight ahead as if he expected or deserved such treatment.

A quarter of a block was traversed before Ruth suddenly, painfully grew up. Furious with her own shortcomings and full of compassion for the man who was fighting her war, who deserved all the best, who badly needed help and instead was receiving treatment that could damage him further, she forced herself to go to him and take his arm, ignoring the hostility surrounding them. Immediately she felt the relief in his tense body. She chattered on to him until a red-faced portly middle-aged man spat "4-F!" at him like a curse.

After a painful silence, and when they were well away from the man, she volunteered, "In the first place, 4-F's can't help it. They aren't medically unfit for service on purpose, you know. Nobody would be." She couldn't conceive of anyone not wanting to fight for America. "In the second place, and most importantly, you certainly aren't one. You're a—why you're a casualty—and a hero!" and her voice softened.

Now that it was out in the open, John began to talk. He spoke eagerly and quickly, telling her in disjointed sentences his travail, the loss of forty-eight of his shipmates, his best friend who survived with him, the welcome he expected but didn't get, his shame, his frustration, his hopes. Much was incomprehensible to her, for he seemed to think she knew those facts, which were still untold, but she instinctively listened. He talked all the way home, even while they were boarding the street cars, even while he was paying the two nickels necessary for their fare. It occurred to her that he might not have the money, but she stopped herself from offering the small change in case that might bruise his fragile ego even more.

Although she was not physically attracted to him at all, she made up her mind to neck with him if he wished—and she hadn't met one man yet who didn't wish to—to make up to him for the tragedy of the sunken ship and the bad treatment he had been getting. From her, too. Especially from her.

As she opened the front door, she asked him to come in for some Postum, looking up innocently into his face.

Suddenly he stood straighter. And he shook his head, regretfully. "No, Ruth."

She was mystified. "Why not?"

"You—you wouldn't understand. You're a nice girl, Ruth—I know you're a nice girl. No, wait," as she started to query him, puzzled. "I want to thank you, Ruth," and the words came out more slowly now. Each one was an effort. "I want to thank you for—for everything. I know what I look like. Believe it or not, I was a sharp dresser before—well before."

"I want to do something for you. What can I send you when I—when I get settled? A gift for you."

"A gift?" Ruth was overwhelmed with guilt. What had she done that was worthy of a gift? She had behaved shamefully. Just because she had forced herself to be civil certainly was no cause for any appreciation—but a gift?

"I don't need a gift," she responded rather sharply. "I didn't do anything."

"Please. It will help me feel better. Please."

"Well—" Ruth loved to give, and she loved to receive. Besides, maybe he was right. Maybe it would make him feel better. "Are you sure you want to?"

"Yes, Ruth. What would you like? Anything at all."

Riddled by guilt, she didn't want to cost him a lot of money, but he was so insistent—and she did love gifts. She racked her brain. Gum! That was certainly cheap enough—a nickel per pack—and she had a hard time finding it now in the stores. She missed chewing it, especially when she was on a diet, which was often. She knew the servicemen could get it easily. "How about gum?" she asked hesitantly. "I would like a package of gum, if that's all right."

He protested. "Gum? Why gum?"

"I like it—and we civilians can't get it."

"Gum? Only gum? What else?"

"Nothing else, John. I really want the gum." He recognized that she was sincere.

"Okay, if that's what you really want—but I'd like to do better for you." He looked helpless and vulnerable, and her heart went out to him in sympathy again.

"You've been great, John, and I would appreciate the gum very much indeed. That would be great, really."

"Okay, then. Goodbye," and he turned awkwardly to go.

Surprising herself, for the first time in her life she turned to a man and asked softly, "Aren't you going to kiss me goodnight?"

He turned back to her, unable to stop himself, and caught her to him with sudden passion. He just stood there, unable to kiss her, holding her tight in his arms, and shaking uncontrollably. His shaking bewildered Ruth, but she instinctively held him as a mother holds a grown child, comforting him. He finally kissed the face she presented him and then buried his face in her shoulder, still shaking.

"Are you all right, John?" She didn't know what to do for him.

"Yes, I—I've got to go now. Goodbye, Ruth. Thanks again." and he ran down the steps as if the enemy were chasing him.

She went in alone, still puzzled and concerned about his shaking. Could he have some sort of tropical disease? But he didn't shake earlier, only when they were saying goodbye. She finally decided that it probably was because of the ordeal he had undergone.

She didn't really expect any gum from the young man—she realized what a peculiar gift it was, and she didn't even think he had her address. She was thrilled and surprised to find a package delivered to her a month later containing an entire carton of gum from John. An entire carton! How marvelous. He must have noted her address when he took her home. But he hadn't included his return address, so she couldn't thank him. And she never did know his last name.

She never forgot him, though.

CHAPTER 8

As Michael wrote to Ruth, he knew that he should write more often. But he didn't know what to say. He certainly didn't feel ready for any commitment, but there definitely was a bond between them. Would Ruth be able to have a "normal" life? Would she be able to have children? He had never before felt any great need for children—never even thought about it—but the possibility of never being able to have any, whether he wanted them or not, was definitely a disquieting prospect. Would she—most importantly—be able to have sex? How could he even think of a woman who couldn't make love? His mother distrusted and hated her, too—and for all the wrong reasons. There was just no way a relationship with Ruth would work.

But he couldn't forget her. And he carried around her dog-eared, crumpled, worn letters with him in his alarmingly bulging wallet. They weren't quite up to the "sugar report" standard of real love letters, but they were all he had.

He signed the one-page V-Mail with "As ever, Michael," after debating between that, "Fondly, Michael," and "Sincerely, Michael." "Love, Michael" was too much right now. He certainly wasn't ready for that. "As ever" seemed to cover it nicely—his feelings, whatever they were, were the same as they had been.

Pete came in to find him sitting on his bunk, folding the V-Mail rather absently, but remembering not to seal it so that the censor wouldn't wreck it by tearing it open. "Your girlfriend? What was her name—Ruth something?"

"Yes. Ruth Braunstein." She certainly was his girlfriend, he conceded to himself.

"Good-looking broad," Pete offered. "Outstanding in a couple of ways, I'd say."

Michael laughed. He couldn't get mad at Pete. As crude as Pete Roffola could get, there was nothing vicious or cutting about his humor, and his dry wit was contagious. He always meant well. Pete was so appealingly homely that the ladies all wanted to mother him. He accepted this homage gratefully and did his best to give value received in return. He was shorter than Michael by some three inches, much stockier, and strong as an ox. His black hair and brown eyes told of his Italian heritage, and his broken nose and assorted scars harkened back to his early years in Butchertown, one of the toughest neighborhoods in San Francisco.

"Say, Mike," Pete was the only one who ever called him that. "Don't mean to get out of line, but did you ever really make time with her? With those tits—wow!" Pete always got out of line.

"No," and this time Michael was short with this friend. "No, I didn't."

"Oh, sorry," and Pete agreeably dropped the subject, but privately wondered. "Say, have you seen my latest pin-up?" He actually wasn't as far from the subject as he meant to be, but Michael proved amenable. He whistled appreciatively.

It was Betty Grable's body, in her bathing suit, face away from the camera, but she was smiling provocatively over her shoulder. The black high heels matched the little bow in her upswept blonde hair.

"What an ass on that broad!" Pete's eyes caressed the page lovingly. "Now, why don't we get something like that to entertain us, huh?"

"Yeah, I read all the time about Rita Hayworth or Marlene Dietrich entertaining the camps. What do we get? Pin ups! By the way, I see you have the pin up of Rita Hayworth in that black lace nightgown. Not bad, buddy."

Suddenly Pete became belligerent. "Say, did you hear that the Postmaster General is banning those luscious Esquire girls from the mails? Some clown by the name of Frank C. Walker." He spit out the "C." "What a pile of horse shit. I tell you—we can't have the real thing. Why the hell can't we have our pin ups?"

"I don't understand that either. Walker is worse than my mother. All our letters have to be censored—I can understand that all right. After all, 'a slip of the lip can sink a ship,' sure. But we shouldn't have to stand for that kind of censorship!"

"Yeah, I thought we were fighting Hitler," and Pete glowered.

Michael mildly added a little fuel to the fire. "I do think the country is going a bit too far. Did you hear what they said about Frank Sinatra?"

"Frannkieee!" and Pete squealed like a star-struck teenager. "What's with him?"

"My cousin in New York wrote that the Education Commissioner there is threatening to press charges against him."

"What the hell for?"

"Now get this—for encouraging truancy because of those thousands of teenage girls who skip school to listen to him sing—and scream 'Frannkieee!" and Michael squealed in his turn. As they both laughed, he added seriously, "The New York Herald Tribune, so my cousin says, said that Congress put out that Frankie and the Lone Ranger—can you imagine, the Lone Ranger—are the—and he quoted, 'are the prime instigators of juvenile delinquency in America.'" They looked at each other.

"We're not fighting a war for Mom and apple pie," Pete finally said. "We're fighting a war for nuts!"

* * *

Michael and Pete considered themselves fortunate to be aboard the "Lady Lex," the affectionate nickname for the most beloved warship of the fleet, as she steamed into the Coral Sea. She was part of the two-carrier group under Rear Admiral Frank Jack Fletcher, along with most of the ships from the group of Australian and American ships called "MacArthur's Navy" (later know as the Seventh Fleet) and three cruisers, H.M.A.S. Australia and Robert and U.S.S. Chicago, and several destroyers under the Australian Rear Admiral J. G. Crace, R.N. They knew that some of the crew had actually been aboard the Lexington since 1927, when she was first commissioned.

The Armed Forces generally saw to it that the men were trained and placed exactly where they were the least talented. Pete, with a natural interest in medicine, was a cook. Michael was lucky, however. Fresh from Communications School, he was well placed in the ship's Radio Room. He had loved to tinker with radios when he was a child. He had even built one from scratch when he was fifteen, using a combination of odds and ends, a crystal, clips, and earphones, which Bridget was always bragging about. His mother even seemed a bit impressed, though she did ask, "You won't be doing that as a career, will you, dear?"

Michael was increasingly bewildered by the confusing, coded messages he gave and received. Although he originally viewed the officers calling the shots (and signals) with awe and respect, believing they all knew what they were doing, he began to suspect SNAPU ("Situation Normal—All Fucked Up") now and again when the officers' reactions began to turn to almost hysterical disbelief.

On May 4, 1942, the Yorktown, the second carrier under Rear Admiral Fletcher, was already bombing the Japanese, who had taken over Tulagi. They didn't do too much damage to the enemy, but the enemy itself committed a blunder that helped the Allies, the first of many blunders—on both sides. Two of the Japanese ships, Shokaku and Zuikaku, were sent to deliver planes to Rabaul on May 2nd in order to save an extra ferrying mission, so that the Japanese were too far away on May 4th to counterattack either the Yorktown or the Lexington.

On May 7th, the same two Japanese carriers sent out planes to search the Coral Sea for their enemy, and the too-eager pilots reported a carrier and a cruiser. The carriers promptly sunk them. Unfortunately for the Japanese, however, they proved to be a fleet oiler and a destroyer, which were leaving after fueling Admiral Fletcher's ships.

Although this saved the unaware Yorktown and Lexington at that time, the crews on those ships heard men screaming and saw men dying, and the water was thickened with oil and blood and bodies. Michael was kept in the Radio Room until he felt dizzy, whether from exhaustion, from excitement, or from terror. He tried to ignore it until his relief took over, and then he lay on his bunk and tried unsuccessfully to sleep.

It was the Allies turn to blunder. A search plan from Yorktown reported "two carriers and four heavy cruisers" about 175 miles away. After the planes had left to attack what they thought was the Japanese striking force, they discovered the pilot's code contact pad had been out of order. They should have been reported as "two heavy cruisers and two destroyers."

The planes from the Yorktown and the Lexington, however, had unbelievable luck resulting from this mistake. They found the light cruiser Shoho and sunk her in exactly ten minutes, which proved to be a record, not only for the Battle of the Coral Sea, but for the entire war. Lexington's dive-bomber commander exuberantly signaled: "Scratch on flattop!" The Japanese were so discouraged by the Shoho's loss that their forces intending to invade Port Moresby were ordered to mill around at a safe distance instead—and their invasion plan was shelved because the wrong flattop was sunk.

Rear Admiral Fletcher detached the Australian Rear Admiral Crace from his command to find and attack the Port Moresby invasion force, gallantly weakening his own carriers' screen to do so. Crace took his two Australian cruisers, U.S.S. Chicago, and several destroyers and enthusiastically beat off thirty-one bombers from Rabaul.

Unfortunately, he also fought off the U.S. Army Air Force B-17's from Townsville, Queensland, which somehow were under the impression that his ships were Japanese.

To add insult to injury, the frustrated Japanese planes claimed to have sunk two battleships and a heavy cruiser.

Since the U.S. B-17's thought Crace's ships were Japanese, the Japanese could do no less. While attempting to find the Lexington and the Yorktown in the dark, six of the Japanese planes found the Yorktown. The only problem was that they thought the Yorktown was Japanese and tried to land on her. Needless to say, they didn't leave.

Scuttlebutt about the two cases of mistaken identity flew around the ship faster than a speeding bullet, and Pete resolved the problem. Since apparently neither the Americans nor the Japanese could tell the ships apart, he suggested that white hats be placed on the Allied ships and black hats on the Axis ships. "That way we all know who we're fighting. The only problem is that they would be helluva big hats."

Michael agreed. "And we know who those big hats would fit, right? I could name a few in Washington." They laughed because they could not cry.

On May 8th, heavy clouds had moved from the Solomon Islands into the Coral Sea, effectively hiding the Japanese. The Americans, under brilliant sunshine, realized this disadvantage and were, accordingly, more nervous than ever. Forty-one planes from the Yorktown missed the Zuikaku in a furious rainstorm, but they did bomb the Shokaku twice, with one of the hits damaging the flight deck so badly that no more planes could be launched. Although half of the planes from the Lexington searched in vain for the enemy so effectively hidden in the mists, the other half bombed the Shokaku.

While the pilots on the attack planes from the Yorktown and the Lexington were frantically chasing the enemy, Japanese torpedoes and bombs were falling indiscriminately on their ships.

Michael was grimly sending messages:

> PLANES SEEM TO BE
> COMPLETELY AROUND US . . .
> FIRE ON WATER OFF OUR PORT
> BEAM . . .
> THAT'S ONE JAP DOWN OFF OUR
> PORT QUARTER NOW . . .
> THEY ARE USING FLARES . . .
> ANOTHER JAP DOWN . . .
> ANOTHER ONE . . .
> ONE SHIP HIT WITH TORPEDO

Someone yelled that the Yorktown had taken a big hit. Michael kept sending as if it were his personal lifeline.

"Need another man to fight this fire here! Michael?" Tom Scanner, a clean-cut tall blonde Boatswain's Mate in his late twenties, blackened almost beyond recognition, had rushed in for help. Michael looked at Joe Luchesi, sitting alongside him, rapidly sending. Joe added a last message, and he and Michael left at a run.

Although the action in the Radio Room was frantic, it had been organized. Outside it was organized chaos. Men were running furiously in all directions in a smoky haze, although they all seemed to know where they were going. The fire seemed to be coming from more than one section. A flame burst free from the smoke to Michael's right and then he noticed another to his left. Suddenly he realized that the desk was sliding sideways under his feet. At first he wondered if he were just dizzy again, but Tom was having trouble keeping his balance too.

"There are three fires on board," Tom gasped. "The ship's listing." His voice rose for a moment, and he pushed down the hysteria. "The power plant's okay though. Has to be." And they were there. Tom handed him the fire-fighting equipment and suddenly was gone.

The smoke almost obscured the flames. Trying his neckerchief about his nose and mouth, Michael concentrated on the fire. Sweat poured down his face, into his eyes, and sparks danced on his dungarees. He knew the power plant was still intact, and it had to remain that way. No matter what, the fire must be extinguished. He wasn't the only one there. There seemed to be others, but he saw only indistinct shadows through the smoke and his blurred vision.

Suddenly, the ship was wracked by an explosion. Then another. Michael was thrown backward, away from the fire. He heard his name called at that moment. He twisted his body to hear better. Was that Pete? It had really sounded like a feminine voice, very like Ruth. But, of course, it couldn't be. He turned a bit more—and he missed the full brunt of the falling bulkhead. One leg only was caught, but the intense pain made him black out.

"Abandon ship! Abandon ship!" The great foghorn of a voice reverberated throughout the ship. Michael opened his eyes to see Ron Acaro and Tony Smith leaning over him in an attempt to free him. He didn't know how long he was out. The two husky sailors were straining to lift the heavy bulkhead off him, but they couldn't seem to quite make it. Ron noticed Michael was conscious and immediately suggested he roll out while they lifted it as high as they could. He nodded. As they lifted, he began rolling over. He began blacking out again but struggled for consciousness and made it.

"Now you can pass out, buddy," Ron murmured softly as they let the bulkhead fall again, with Michael in the clear. Michael obligingly passed out.

As the two men began carrying Michael, he opened his eyes again. "Any corpsman around?" he inquired weakly.

"I've called 'Corpsman!' for any kind of medical aid until I'm hoarse," Tony replied crisply. "We'll just get you over the side into safety."

Just then Pete came up from below with a group of men, all carefully carrying their helmets.

"Pete!" he called, but his voice was so weak it didn't carry.

"Hey, Pete!" reinforced Ron, and Pete, concerned for his friend, left the others to run to Michael's side.

"You okay?" Michael was relieved that Pete hadn't been hurt.

"Sure, Mike. You got hit a bit, huh?"

"Not too bad," Michael responded with a grimace. He was feeling better. "It might be a thousand-dollar wound—maybe even a million-dollar one!" A thousand-dollar wound would get him out of the battle; a million-dollar one would get him out of the war. "Why are you taking off your shoes? Oh, we're going over the side, of course." He answered his own question.

"Captain Sherman wants us to put our shoes in order," and Pete carefully took Michael's off for him, adding them to the orderly row of shoes on the flight deck. Ron and Tony began carrying Michael to the basket stretcher, with Pete alongside, still carrying his helmet.

"What's that you guys are carrying in your helmets?" grunted Tony as they made their way aft.

Pete showed it to him.

All the men began to laugh, even Michael. "Ice cream? You guys are carrying ice cream?"

"Sure. Good stuff. Want some?" Tony and Ron helped themselves, still laughing, while Pete made sure Michael had a good mouthful just before he was helped into the basket stretcher. Ron and Tony slid down a line over the side, with Pete close behind.

Rear Admiral Frederick C. Sherman, the Lexington's captain, proudly issued the statement much later: "At sunset, in a very orderly fashion, the men—reluctantly—were taken off to destroyers and cruisers. They were so calm that some of them went below and filled their helmets with ice cream from the ship's stores and went over the side eating. All arranged their shoes in an orderly row on the flight deck before leaving. No lives were lost at all in the water. All our casualties came from combat or fire fighting."

Michael watched the Lady Lex go down in silence, as did his shipmates. She had to be sunk by a friendly destroyer's torpedoes. Tears filled his eyes, and he turned his head to hide them. He didn't know that he wasn't the only one grieving for a good ship.

Later Michael found out that, although the Lexington's loss gave the Japanese the winning score in tonnage sunk, the battle was won by the Americans. The Japanese were afraid of risking the Port Moresby Invasion Force without air protection and ordered that to retire to Rabaul—and all because the Americans originally made their biggest mistake, the sighting and bombing of Shoho, which caused the Japanese to retreat. An extra bonus was that the Shokaku took two months to repair and the Zuikaku took over one month to replace her lost planes, which effectively kept them out of the war for that time period.

CHAPTER 9

Ruth was tired on May 7th. She had a feeling of general malaise, a foreboding she couldn't quite identify. Her mother, always concerned about her, wasn't too alarmed. Ruth frequently was tired.

She went to bed about 8:00, early even for her. At first she was restless, tossing and turning, at last falling asleep, but it was an uneasy sleep, haunted by senseless bits of dreams and visions. The dream seemed to turn into a scene at the store, in which she was endlessly waiting on one perennially dissatisfied customer, when suddenly her dream was interrupted. The customer's face turned into Michael's, and clearly he was in great danger. They weren't in the store anymore; they were somewhere else, somewhere where the horizon stretched out limitlessly in all directions. She had to warn him. She had tell him to watch out—"Michael! Michael!"

She woke up screaming. Her parents, both in their nightclothes, wasted no time running to her room.

Etta gasped first, "What is it? What's the matter, Ruth?" with Max behind her, more befogged by sleep than his wife.

Ruth was sitting up in bed, frozen. She regained control slowly and attempted to make light of it to save her parents further worry. "Just a bad dream, I guess. That was a dream. Just a dream." She was trying to talk herself into reality.

Max, grunting, began going back to bed, but Etta stayed on for a moment. "A bad dream? A nightmare. What was it about, Ruth?"

"Oh, Michael was in danger somehow, and I was trying to warn him," Ruth responded slowly, and then realized that any dreaming about Michael was not going to be appreciated or approved by either of her parents. "It was nothing," and she lay back down again. "I'm sorry it disturbed you. Just a dream."

Now that Ruth was all right and that the entire commotion had been caused by someone miles away that Etta had hoped Ruth was forgetting, Etta was annoyed and showed it. "So, just a dream. Do you realize, young lady that it's near midnight? Go to sleep and forget that young man." She began leaving, then turned at the door to say in a softer tone, "Go to sleep, honey. You need your sleep."

Ruth was wide awake. She glanced at her small alarm clock by the bed. Her mother was right, it was near midnight. What a terrible dream—no, not really a dream, more like a sensation. She was alarmed in every bone in her body, and telling herself it was just a dream didn't do too much good. It wasn't like any other dream she had ever had. It had even interrupted a real dream. Tears began to run down her cheeks. What if Michael really was in danger? Of course the war itself was dangerous—but what was happening to Michael? She closed her wet eyes tightly and began to pray. She didn't know what else to do. She prayed for God to look after Michael and keep him safe—not necessarily to bring him home to her, she didn't want to ask for too much at once—but just to keep him safe.

She had heard from him just yesterday. His letters were becoming less stilted, less formal. She had glimpsed something in his last letter that elated her, gave her hope. He had even signed it "Fondly,

Michael," which was a bit of an improvement over "As ever." Nothing could have happened to him. She remembered John with a pang—that couldn't happen to Michael.

Two days later she heard over the radio that on May 8th a battle in the Coral Sea had involved a carrier taskforce, which saved Port Moresby from invasion by the Japanese. One of the carriers, the Lexington, had been sunk with minimum casualties. The Lexington! Michael had spoken affectionately of the Lady Lex. It was his ship.

She was devastated. And she remembered her "dream" very well. The timing between that "dream" and the reality of tragedy was all off, but Michael had been in danger.

She knew Mrs. Stratton wouldn't give her any information, so she immediately telephoned Sally and asked her to find out what she could at the USO. Sally, very excited and yet concerned, did find out that Mrs. Stratton's son had been aboard the Lexington and seemed to be worried about him.

Ruth waited for the mail and prayed a great deal. That was all she could do.

CHAPTER 10

The Naval Hospital at New Caledonia was starched and shining white, and the nurse who marched into Michael's room matched the décor, even to her white hair. As Michael lay in bed, watching her bustle around, he wondered idly how such an old nurse got into the Navy. She looked at least forty, with wrinkles to match, though her hair probably was prematurely white. With all the beautiful young nurses he had glimpsed passing in the halls, he was stuck with this one. Not that he'd know what to do with a beautiful young nurse if he had one, he thought ironically. His sexual drive wasn't noticeably diminished by his crushed leg, which now, encased in a spotless cast, hurt like hell, but he still was a virgin. Besides, nurses were officers' meat. Everyone knew that.

She was competent, of course. She had introduced herself as Lieutenant Plant. If she expected him to salute her from the bed, she was going to be disappointed, he thought perversely. He could always please illness.

"Well, everything is shipshape here now for you, ahh—" She checked the chart. "Petty Officer Radioman Third Class Stratton." He thought that the only thing she omitted was his blood type, but he thanked her.

"Your nurse, Ensign Sabrella, should be here shortly," and she tested the windowsill for dust and left.

His nurse? Oh, of course. A lieutenant would be a head nurse. Good. Well, let's see what the luck of the draw would bring.

He gazed idly out of the window. He was the only one in the ward as yet, though the beds were made and ready. The pills didn't seem to do too much for the pain. Although they had put a cast on the entire leg already, he didn't know how bad it was yet. God, he hoped he'd still have the use of it—even limping would be better than—he broke off the thought.

The view from the window was beautiful. He watched the waves break against the shore, the white foam rolling over and over against itself. The hospital was on Anse Vata Beach, a little way out from Noumea, and the view was of the peaceful Pacific. Although the Pacific wasn't so peaceful the last time he saw it, it seemed to help heal him now.

His thoughts were of Ruth. Except for when he we fighting the fire (thank God everyone had to go to firefighting school), he seemed to be always thinking of Ruth. Even when he was fighting the fire—who was that who called to him—and saved his life? He definitely heard the call. It certainly sounded like Ruth, but that was impossible. Maybe it was Pete with his voice distorted somehow by excitement or fright. He'd have to ask him when he came to see him.

He mused wryly that it was the first time he had seen the Bosun's Mate without a cup of coffee in his hand. He must have run out of deck apes to command to ask him to help with that fire. What happened to him, anyway? And with everything, the Lady Lex, the beautiful wonderful Lady Lex was irretrievably lost—but the Japanese weren't able to sink her. No, one of our own destroyers did the dirty deed. Neither Michael nor his shipmates were ashamed of the tears that blurred their eyes when they watched the torpedoes kill that gallant Lady.

He had heard scuttlebutt through the grapevine already that the Yorktown lost sixty-six in that hit, but she was still afloat. Well, Lady Lex may have been sunk, but she went out proudly. He had heard that he was one of 150 wounded that were lowered in orderly fashion in basket stretchers into motor whaleboats. Pete and the other able-bodied slid down on lines into the water and were picked up by destroyers.

Ruth, Ruth, Ruth. He had to live (with two good legs, preferably) for Ruth. He reluctantly came to the decision that he must love her, despite the obvious problems. And please God she would be—be normal. He couldn't think of a better word, though he hated that one.

He wished he had some writing materials so he could write to her. When his nurse did come in, he'd ask.

When his nurse finally entered, confidently swinging into the room with a graceful, fluid motion, all thoughts of the letter were swept from his mind by the easy roll of her hips. In fact, he momentarily forgot all about Ruth. His luck was fantastically good. Ensign Sabrella was a tall slender young woman a few years older than he, with large brown Latin eyes, short curly black hair, a full generous mouth, and a spectacular figure, even in the prim uniform. His eyes slowly traveled down and then up from the sensible white shoes. Her long shapely legs were terrific. Her breasts, though not overly large, were beautifully and separately shaped, with the tiny waist emphasizing the soft curve of her hips. Completely unselfconscious, her body was sensual and inviting, even with the few stains on the almost white uniform. Her face was pretty, though a bit hard. He caught his breath and gazed at her wistfully, longingly.

She knew just what kind of a sensation she caused, and she enjoyed it. She smiled in sympathy, in understanding. Her tone, however, was proper and formal, though with an intriguing Texas drawl. "Hello. I'm Ensign Sabrella—and you are—?" She was looking straight into his eyes. She didn't even glance at his chart.

"Michal Stratton, ma'am." He wouldn't mind saluting. With everything he had.

"Glad to meet you, Michael," she smiled, and her voice became softer, more seductive. "And you may call me Rita—in private—if you like."

She had noticed the broad shoulders, the deep blue eyes, and the rugged masculinity of the man. Too many of the officers she came into contact with her were slight, effeminate little men, who spoke of little more than the great jobs they were doing and how much office work it took to conduct the war. She was certainly aware that she shouldn't fraternize with enlisted men, of course, but Rita Sabrella was a born rebel.

Michael couldn't believe what was happening. He told himself that she probably was just normally friendly, that he was imagining a fantasy come true—but her eyes! Their message was loud and clear. Maybe she was just a flirt with everyone, though. He had better proceed cautiously. She was an officer, after all, and he could be in deep trouble if he misunderstood.

"Thank you—uhh—ma'am," he managed.

Again, she smiled in understanding. "Now what can I do to make a big handsome sailor boy comfortable?" She straightened up his already straight blanket and then, deliberately, slowly, held him to her full breasts while she fluffed up his pillow, both of them close together under the rolled up mosquito netting. He couldn't misunderstand. And neither could she. The one thin blanket and sheet didn't hide a thing.

If this kept on, she would have to change the sheets, he thought bemusedly. She certainly didn't waste any time. He was still unsure, however. Was she this way with everyone, or was he just irresistible? He always had been the chaser; he wasn't sure he liked being the chase. Or did it matter? It seemed to be a golden opportunity. He'd be a fool to resist. The danger inherent in fraternization between officer and enlisted man would only add spice.

He tentatively reached for her hand. She not only allowed him to take it, but squeezed his hand warmly with hers. No mistake. All signals were go.

"How did I get so lucky?" He smiled, completely aroused. "A beautiful girl like you. You're the nurse of my dreams." That was certainly the truth. He was more than ready. No time like the present. No one else was around—he could ignore his bad leg. He was certain that somehow she could arrange to concentrate on the other two. He began moving over in the bed, pulling his bad leg with him. He smiled his most devastating smile and looked up meaningfully into her lovely Latin eyes, opening the blanket invitingly.

Then he remembered his condoms. The girl was obviously <u>not</u> a virgin. The training films with their graphic illustrations of what happened to those unfortunates with advance venereal disease made him season his need and his haste with a dash of caution. He might really need a condom with her. He reached for his wallet in the nightstand, realizing that his wallet was somewhere on the bottom of the Pacific, and the door opened.

Lieutenant Plant and two other nurses were ushering in the wounded men on stretchers to fill up the empty beds. They were no longer alone. He felt a sharp ache in his groin and equally sharp disappointment. He lay back down, suddenly exhausted.

"We can do that another time, sailor," Rita spoke formally again, in perfect control of herself, though her eyes sparkled with delight. She had no intention of bedding the sailor now. She knew Lieutenant Plant was due in at any time. She did enjoy danger, but she wasn't stupid. But another time—

"Now what else would you like at the moment? You have your water, I see. Do you have a bedpan?"

"Yes." What a hell of a note to end on.

"Nothing else, then?" And Rita began to leave him to help with the newly arrived men.

He suddenly remembered. "Writing materials, if you have them. I'd appreciate that." He felt a twinge of guilt as he spoke, but he also enjoyed the fact that he could respond with that particular request.

Rita just nodded and produced paper and pen from her pockets for him, writing "See you later" in a strong, large hand across the top sheet and smiling at him. He smiled back in anticipation. All was not lost, then.

Rita Sabrella then helped the other men with the menial tasks assigned to her as Lieutenant Plant and the other nurses left; reminiscing to herself about the unusual choice she had made to become a Navy nurse.

Her family came from good Spanish stock—aristocracy, actually, and she had always held her head high. But her father had fought with his elder brother, the rightful heir, over something quite inconsequential. He was certain he was right and proudly left Castille and his family with Carmelita, his pregnant bride, who had been impregnated on her wedding night, for the New World. He had quite enough money on his own to become one of the large landowners in Texas, and, when oil was found on his land, he was gratified—for then he surpassed his brother, despite the title.

When Rita was born, the youngest and only girl after Carmelita Sabrella had given birth to seven boys; no one could deny her anything. Rita was a natural flirt, and her sweetness and beauty made her irresistible to all the men in the family. Even Carmelita spoiled her.

Carmelita had rebelled too, however. After her eighth child, she was still attractive. She was in her early thirties and had a strong sex drive. And she loved her husband deeply. Though she also loved every one of her children dearly, she definitely did not want any more babies. So she rebelled against the church. She took precautions, though she confessed very privately, in her own mind, every time she went to Mass. After all, the church was much opposed against such precautions, and she certainly didn't want to be excommunicated.

After Rita graduated from college, she decided to take up nursing, which was a rather unconventional choice for a well-bred young lady in her circle. Her parents tolerantly excused her choice by saying that would make her a good mother in later years. She could have her pick of any man in the territory, not only for her money, but for her beauty, her open sensuality. When she announced she wanted to join the

Navy, the United States Navy, everyone was shocked. They told her that she wouldn't have a maid in the Navy, that she would have to work hard, that she would have to do dirty, menial work like emptying bed pans, and—most important—that she would be in danger. How could she do this to them? With all their tears and wringing of hands, she did exactly what she wanted, as usual, and they forgave her, as usual, though they still worried about her.

Rita wanted to go in the Navy because it was adventurous, thrilling—and all those men! She used birth control all the time, and it didn't bother her a bit. She considered it a private matter between herself and her own conscience, and her conscience was silent on the subject. Though she did go to Mass regularly, too. Habit was strong.

The actuality wasn't as thrilling as the idea, however. There were grievously hurt men here, dying men, and sometimes she was their only comfort. It was a large responsibility for a wealthy, spoiled young lady who hadn't bothered to even pick up her own room at home. But Rita Sabrella was not only a natural flirt. She was also a natural nurse. She discovered she enjoyed taking care of the men, alleviating suffering where she could, helping those who needed help, and instilling hope into those who had no hope. She was a gracious lady in her own way.

The men were a bonus. The officers, of course, usually fell all over themselves for her, and she would have been surprised if they had not, but they did not come up to her expectations. And, though she hated to admit it, being without a maid had its disadvantages. She never did get used to doing her own laundry, and

Lieutenant Plant was always criticizing her for not being immaculate.

But when Rita Sabrella wanted something, anything, she was not to be denied.

CHAPTER 11

Ruth woke up on Tuesday feeling great. Somehow she knew that Michael was safe and that she would hear from him very soon. The news of the Richfield Reporter on the radio last night had not been especially disturbing, but that was not the reason she felt so confident. She felt it in the depths of her soul, and she ventured to peek again at the Argyle stockings she was lovingly knitting for him. Ruth was not a particularly adroit knitter—or seamstress, for that matter. It was one of Etta Braunstein's disappointments that her own expertise in sewing did not reflect itself in her daughter. The stockings, with their intricate triangles and lines in bright yellows and blues, and reds, looked odd indeed. No matter how closely Ruth followed the complicated instructions, the pattern never came out as it was supposed to. The straight lines had taken on a life of their own which was not particularly straight, and the triangles were definitely lopsided. She sighed and began dressing for work. Apparently love was not enough to create beauty—at least in stockings.

She was so confident that she would hear from Michael that she was tempted to play sick and stay home so that she could get the mail as soon as it arrived, but she went to work, mainly because she didn't want to jinx any good luck by counting it before it really happened.

When Mrs. Kaminsky dropped into the store to buy a new purse, Ruth greeted her cheerfully. Madeline Kaminsky was Ruth's favorite customer and a good friend; a short, round, bustling individual with frankly gray hair, smooth white skin, and bright and intelligent brown eyes. She and Ruth had become friends almost at once when they first met at the store months ago. They confided in each other as if they had known one another for years, almost as if she were a girlfriend, although she was older than Ruth's mother. Although they never saw each other outside of the store, Ruth knew all about her and her husband and her tragic inability to bear children, and in turn, she knew all about Michael and Ruth's worries about him, and she responded to the girl with a smile that transformed her into a pretty woman.

"You've heard from Michael?" She greeted Ruth with an affectionate hand on her arm.

"No, Mrs. Kaminsky, not yet. But—but I feel that I will. Does that make sense?" And Ruth laughed a little at the absurdity.

Mrs. Kaminsky looked at her oddly. "Why, yes, Ruth, it does. It really does," she repeated to herself slowly. Madeline Kaminsky sympathized whole-heartedly with Ruth and often wished she could help her. At last she knew she could. She should have known there was a good reason for their rapport.

She hesitated a moment, not looking at Ruth, absentmindedly fingering her wedding ring. She seemed to have difficulty framing what she wanted to say, finally blurting out, "You—you're going to hear from Michael tonight, you know."

Both women had forgotten completely about the purse Mrs. Kaminsky had come in to buy.

Ruth was surprised. "Yes, I have a feeling I will, too. But how did you know?"

Again Mrs. Kaminsky hesitated. "I haven't mentioned this before, because I didn't know whether or not you would understand. But now I know somehow that you will. I am—intuitive. And so are you."

"No, I'm not a fortune teller," Mrs. Kaminsky responded softly. "And, no, I can't read minds," she went on, apparently reading Ruth's mind. "I am a bit psychic, though—and so are you. It just came to me. You're going to get what you want, you know. Just be careful it's what you really want." Her honest brown eyes were candid as they met Ruth's puzzled green eyes.

Ruth smiled uncertainly. "I'm not sure what you mean."

"Aren't you?"

And suddenly Ruth did know. It was if she had known all along, but had to be reminded.

She was fascinated and she had to know more. She glanced at her watch. "Good, it's my lunch time. Could we—" She didn't have to finish.

Mrs. Kaminsky nodded her head briskly, as eager as Ruth to pursue the subject. "Certainly we can lunch together. It'll be great—and a bit more private. I'll wait for you to get your things."

"I'll be ready in a minute." And Ruth ran breathlessly to fetch her coat and purse, feeling grateful that her replacement was already there and calling to her as she went by. Contrary to tradition, she didn't wear either hat or gloves to work as the older women did. She had brought her lunch in a brown paper bag as usual, but she would just save it until tomorrow. She knew she had a dollar and some change in her purse, which would be plenty for her to treat Mrs. Kaminsky. The sandwiches at the little coffee shop on the corner were about a quarter each, and coffee or tea was a nickel, of course, so that left her plenty to spare, even considering the ten percent tip and the nickel she had to save for her carfare.

They managed to find a fairly private booth in a corner of the coffee shop, and Madeline Kaminsky began telling Ruth, as quietly as possible, about her psychic experience. Both realized that if the wrong people were to hear, ridicule would be the least of their problems. In 1942 only the "crackpots" believed in psychic phenomenon.

"I guess it was a gradual process," she began. "I remember a few isolated instances years ago, though. I knew when my brother passed on before I was told. I loved him very much. I still do," and to both her own and Ruth's dismay, her eyes filled with tears. She wiped her eyes and kept going, determined not to break down. "It was years ago, hon, I don't know why I still—well, anyway," and she cleared her throat and continued, "I also heard my mother's voice once when it interrupted a dream. She was calling me urgently, and it woke me up at 4:00 in the morning. At the time, she was in Poland, while I was in San Francisco. I wrote her about it and found out she had had a bad dream at 2:00 in the afternoon while she was napping. That's 4:00 a.m. our time, Ruth. She had dreamt that I was hurt and was calling me—exactly as I had heard it. Lots of little things like that. I just took them for granted when I was young, before I really got into this. Seems like a million years ago now."

Madeline Kaminsky hadn't been looking directly at Ruth. She was reliving her past, gazing into the distance, when she suddenly looked at Ruth's face. She interrupted herself sharply. "What is it, Ruth?"

Ruth could barely speak. Her dream about Michael! And the time change—she had forgotten about that. What time was it—nearly midnight on the 7th of May? She remembered her mother mentioning the time. The battle of the Coral Sea—that had been on May 8th, she remembered.

"Mrs. K-K-Kaminsky," Ruth stuttered in her eagerness. "I-I think I may have had an experience like that. Tell me, it's important—tell me, do you know the time difference between different places in the world —like between the Coral Sea and San Francisco?" She held her breath waiting for the answer.

"I think I have that on my little address book," Mrs. Kaminsky responded slowly, aware of the importance of the question, and looking in her oversized purse. It took her a few minutes to find the address book, while both women were silent. "Oh, here it is, under my wallet. Let's see and she rifled through the tiny pages. "Yes, yes, I have it, Ruth. What time do you want to know about?"

"Nearly midnight on May 7th—please." Ruth felt as if she might pass out from the suspense, and she let her breath out slowly.

Mrs. Kaminsky was excited, too, but she forced herself to look carefully at the time differentials. "Let's see." She seemed to be in slow motion both to herself and to Ruth. "That would cross the International Date Line. The Coral Sea would be the nearest to—oh, yes, Sydney, Australia. That would be on May 8th, a day later, and about—oh, just about 6:00 p.m." Then she looked up slowly. "That's it, isn't it, Ruth? That's the battle of the Coral Sea—I heard about it on the radio. And you told me Michael was on the Lexington, of course."

"Yes, oh, yes." And then the waitress came to take their order.

Mrs. Kaminsky recovered first. "I believe I'd like a turkey sandwich and a cup of tea, please. How about you, Ruth?" She had scarcely looked at the menu, but knew that it would be more or less standard fare.

Ruth nodded. "I'll take the same, please," and both smiled brightly at the middle-aged, peroxide blonde who was standing waiting at their booth.

As she wrote down the order, Mrs. Kaminsky laughed nervously. "I guess we must be compatible. Do you like turkey, too?"

"Yes, it's pretty good." Ruth did like turkey, but she wasn't about to waste any time thinking about what to order.

The waitress nodded and left. And now the words tumbled out of Ruth.

When she finished telling the older woman about her dream of Michael in danger, which interrupted the ordinary dream about the store, and how she was warning him, and how the times were exact, now that she remembered about the time change, and how now she knew he was out of danger, her green eyes were no longer puzzled. They were full of awe and wonderment.

"It's better than I had hoped," Mrs. Kaminsky responded eagerly. "You are definitely psychic, Ruth. Or should I say 'intuitive'?" And they both smiled.

Ruth began remembering other 'odd' experiences. "I've never thought of myself as psychic before, but I usually know when my girlfriend Sally is going to phone me. And once when I was little I knew my mother was real sick before they told me. I was outside playing, and suddenly I just knew it. I guess I was about five or six. I ran inside, and my brother David told me she was ill and had to go to the hospital while I stayed with a neighbor. I found out later she had a heart attack. She's all right now, though."

They sat in silence for a moment, and then both began to speak at once, and then both were interrupted by the waitress bringing their order.

They waited until she left. "Go ahead, Ruth," Mrs. Kaminsky smiled. "You go first. Let's not have that 'age before beauty' routine!"

Ruth had been about to protest, but the quip threw her off balance, and she laughed. She had not response for that, so she gave in. "I just wanted to say that I thought I knew you. I had no idea! This whole idea is so—so fascinating." And she wanted to hear more from this fascinating woman. "Please go on."

Mrs. Kaminsky beamed. "And I just wanted to say that maybe, after all these years, I can have someone read for me for a change."

"Someone read to you?"

"No, no, hon. Read for me. Have you ever heard of psychometry? No? Have you taken chemistry? Yes?" Ruth was shaking her head and nodding in turn, and Mrs. Kaminsky continued. "You know what atoms are, right? Well, the theory is that the little circle of the atoms that intertwine catch vibrations—now I don't know if that's right or not, but that's the theory behind it, anyway. The one who 'reads' the jewelry or keys or anything belonging to the person can feel the vibrations, sometimes past, some-times present, sometimes future. And sometimes I can't tell the difference. It has to be something that the individual has worn for a long time," she cautioned. "Nothing that has ever belonged to anyone else or the vibrations could get mixed up."

"Gee," breathed Ruth. "How interesting. Would you—could you—"

"Certainly," Mrs. Kaminsky promptly agreed. "I'll not only read for you, but I'll teach you to read for me, if you like."

Again, Ruth had the strange feeling that she was just being reminded of these wonders that she had somehow known all this before.

"It will have to be somewhere more private than this, of course. We'll make some arrangements for you to come over to my house this week—perhaps even tomorrow?"

"Oh, yes, I'd love to, Mrs. Kaminsky. Does—does your husband understand?'

Mrs. Kaminsky smiled. "Very much so, very much so. He's very psychic, and he reads too. We occasionally read for friends or for someone in need, but we're too close to read for each other. I'm really very fortunate. I could have a married a man who wouldn't believe in all this, which would have been terrible."

"I think rather he's fortunate, too," Ruth shyly offered.

"Why, thank you, my dear. But to continue." Mrs. Kaminsky was all too aware that Ruth's lunch-time was short. "Suddenly I knew how I could help you. Reading for you would be great, yes—but that's not what I meant. I can help you best by helping you to know yourself better," and she leaned forward, serious and intense. "You can help yourself."

"How? What can I do?" Ruth was confused.

Mrs. Kaminsky took a deep breath. "Do you believe in God, Ruth?"

Ruth's green eyes took on a wary look. Of all people, certainly Mrs. Kaminsky wouldn't try to convert her! "Of course, I do, Mrs. Kaminsky."

Mrs. Kaminsky steadfastly went on, afraid that if she stopped she couldn't continue. "You're absolutely right. God is everywhere, all around, in you, in me. And He wants the best for all of us. He has given all of us psychic power, some more, some less. And you have more than most, Ruth. You can help yourself by following your own intuition. That's God talking to you. Don't ignore it. It's real, and it won't steer you wrong. If you have any feelings about anything at all—listen to them. The more you use them, the better and more reliable they'll be—and they can be invaluable. And another thing, Ruth," and Mrs. Kaminsky leaned forward, brown eyes intent and anxious in her effort to emphasize her words. "I know you, and I know you look on the bright side. You have a great natural positive attitude. Keep that up. If you feel you can succeed, you will succeed—in anything you want to do. It's so important, Ruth, to always expect the best in life, no matter what." She sat back, finished and emotionally drained.

Ruth stared. She digested the information slowly. It was so simple. And she knew it was right. She slowly began to eat the turkey sandwich, which had lain uneaten on her plate, while thinking furiously. Of course. Why hadn't she known that before? Or had she? She felt a deep sense of gratitude and affection for Mrs. Kaminsky. She knew how difficult it must have been for her. "Thank you so much for telling me. I do appreciate it."

Mrs. Kaminsky smiled. "I know, hon. It will be easier for you now, I think. In fact, I know it," and she bent to her sandwich, too.

Ruth regretfully looked at her watch. "I have to run. Let me—"

Mrs. Kaminsky shook her head briskly. "Absolutely not. My treat. I've enjoyed our lunch so much, I insist. It's so rare that I meet somebody else psychic. Here I want to give you my address," and she scribbled her address and phone number on the unused paper napkin. "About 7:30 tomorrow night all right?"

Ruth began to argue. "Of course 7:30 is fine, but this is my treat, please. After all—"

Mrs. Kaminsky out-argued her. "No, no, Ruth. After I read for you, I'm going to teach you to read for me—that will be such a pleasure for me that you can't deny me this."

Ruth couldn't wait any longer. She gulped down the last bite of her sandwich, smiled, put on her coat, and dropped a kiss on the older woman's forehead. "Well, you stay and finish your sandwich. I'll see you tomorrow. I hate to leave, but I've got to get back to work. And thank you—for everything."

That night Ruth received five letters from Michael.

CHAPTER 12

Michael tried to turn over in bed to face Pete, with unfortunate results. "Screw this damn leg, anyway!" he grunted with deep feeling and rolled back on his back, grimacing with pain.

Pete only murmured, "Not my type, kid. Now <u>some</u> legs . . ."

Those men in the ward that could laugh did, and even Michael had to grin. Pete was a good for him. He had come to visit him at least four times a week, as often as he could get away from the receiving station, where they put his cooking talents to work while he was awaiting reassignment.

"Say, Pete," and Michael turned toward him again, but only his head this time. "I keep forgetting to ask you. When the roof fell in on me, did you call? I definitely heard someone call "Michael" just before it happened, and I turned a bit to see who it was. Was that you?"

Pete shook his head. "No way, buddy. I was down getting my ice cream just before we left, and I sure didn't have any time for that. I didn't see you at all. I thought you were in the Radio Room."

Michael was silent. "That's odd. I really think it saved my life, whoever called. If I hadn't turned at that moment, it would have fallen on my head, I think."

"I'm going to keep you as a buddy, friend. Anyone who's on a personal basis with God is my kind of guy! Does He talk to you often?"

Laughter again erupted in the ward, and Michael was a bit embarrassed, though he grinned too. "Hey, Pete—in the first place, it was a girl's voice, and—"

"What? Do you mean to say you mistook my basso profundo for a girl's voice?" and Pete deliberately spoke in a high-pitched squeal. He saw Michael's embarrassment however, and began to change the subject when he saw it wasn't necessary, because Rita chose that moment to swing in and out. Both men's eyes followed her avidly, as did the entire ward, after which they discussed her in detail.

After Pete left, Michael felt completely alone, despite the presence of the other wounded men. God damn it, but the weeks were long lying here. He wrote to Ruth constantly, to Bridget regularly, and even to his mother and his aunt and uncle in New York occasionally, but no letters from any of them or anyone else had found their way to him yet, though he was reasonably sure Ruth was writing.

He felt completely confused, too, about his growing feelings for Ruth and his equally growing feelings for Rita, which were the same and yet very different. There was no way that anything could be done about Rita, anyway, with the ward full and he practically chained to the bed with that huge cast.

The only good thing that had happened was that he was told casually by a corpsman who looked about sixteen that he was going to keep his leg, which was broken in three places, that he was damn lucky, that it was healing nicely, but that he might limp, that it was at least a thousand-dollar wound which would keep him out of the fighting for the moment, and that it might even be a million-dollar one which would actually get him home, and didn't anyone tell him that yet?

He was lucky. The Boatswain's Mate had been killed by shrapnel—just one tiny piece of shrapnel.

Through the head. Tom Scanner left a wife and three children. Nice looking family. Michael had seen their photos often enough.

Yes, he was a lucky bastard. Why did he feel so miserable?

CHAPTER 13

Catherine Stratton checked the invitation list for the party for the last time and tossed it aside. "I wonder if the Roosevelts will actually come—we did know Eleanor years ago, you know," she said to her husband, who was reading the New York Times in their elegant Park Avenue brownstone in the city of New York.

"He is a busy man," Bill Stratton drawled slowly, not lifting his eyes from the paper, "and we only met her once at that party about twenty years ago—it was before Franklin became President. Do you know," and he lowered the paper. "It seems as if Roosevelt is always the President and Joe Louis is always the boxing champion. Well, I guess it keeps the stocks stabilized."

"Wouldn't it be great if they did come, though?" she murmured dreamily.

"Don't count on it." He lifted his paper again. "You know, parties aren't really the 'in' thing, with all the money needed for the war effort. Some people might think we're unpatriotic— including the Roosevelts."

"Twenty-five whole years of a good marriage certainly deserves a good party!" she replied heatedly. "And you know I've made it as economical as I can! And with all that you have contributed to war bonds and to helping—"

"Okay, okay." He waved a hand to ward off her protests and looked at her fondly. "Yes, it's a good marriage, Cath. A quarter of a century—that's a long time and does deserve an anniversary celebration. It'll probably be fine even with the Roosevelts—I know they have a few parties of their own. What made you invite them anyway?"

She replied pertly. "Why shouldn't I? We're having the elite, aren't we? We've always had the best people—I just thought I'd update the list a bit and add a few new ones. Besides the usual, I've invited the Roosevelts, the Vanderbilts, the Sabrellas, and the Kennedys."

"Well!" The paper went down again. "Well I hope for your sake that all of them accept—but I doubt it. For instance, you have heard that Joe Kennedy is in England, busy being Ambassador, haven't you?"

"Of course. But some of his family is here at the moment," she replied smugly. "Besides it would be such a feather in our caps to have any of them here. Wouldn't it, Bill?"

Bill Stratton smiled at his attractive wife, still smart looking, and her sleek blonde hair still without a sign of gray. He hoped they would accept for her sake. These society things were so important to her. He had more than enough contact with high society in his brokerage firm, but he would rather work than party. He had become president by dint of hard work, not because of his family or his money, and that was his main pleasure. That and pleasing his wife. And the girls, of course. Bill was a family man.

"Yes, dear, it certainly would. Who else are we having?" And the paper went up again. "How about the family?"

"Oh, yes, we're having family and family and family." She sighed happily. "Even the girls are able to come—with their husbands, of course." Their three daughters were their pride—and sometimes their aggravation. For one thing, their choice of husbands had been peculiar, to say the least—all three of them. But it was their choice, and Bill and Catherine, although privately a bit unhappy about all three choices made the best of it and publicly praised their sons-in-law as lavishly as they could without feeling hypocritical. Maybe the song was right, "The gravy's in the Navy," and the cream was in the Armed Forces. The ones that were left did seem either "too young or too old." And sometimes Catherine wondered if any men that their precious girls would marry would have satisfied them —and that thought helped.

"Even Nancy and what's his name?" Bill was smiling.

"Come on, Bill. His name is Anatoly Yurgilevic, and you know it." Catherine was reproachful. "Yes, even as pregnant as she is, she'll be here."

"Our first grandchild. And from our youngest. Isn't nineteen a bit young to bear children, Cath?" He frowned now, folding the paper up neatly.

"I was nineteen. Remember?"

"Well, that was different. She couldn't finish college! And that damn fortune hunter has to be the father!" His naturally flushed face reddened even more, and his fists clenched in his frustration at his favorite daughter's situation.

"Bill, Bill. Not that again! He's trying to find a position he'll be comfortable in. He is looking."

"While we're paying! He didn't like the brokerage house, did he? And the only position he'll be comfortable in is sitting on his ass!"

Catherine had to laugh. Bill was probably right.

Of all their sons-in-law, Anatoly was the one most typical of the stereotyped European playboy.

"Are you inviting my miserable sister-in-law again?" Bill's good mood had evaporated.

Catherine's tone was calm and placating. Bill was a big man, in all respects, floridly handsome—and his blood pressure was on the high side. "I just don't know, Bill. She certainly would come running, all the way from California. But—" and she hesitated.

"You don't have to, you know. Just because my brother made a mistake years ago doesn't mean we always have to invite her to our parties." He deliberately unfolded the paper again.

"Well—I suppose I should. But do you know what she said when I gave her that jade bracelet for her birthday?" And then she added rather sharply, "Which was very nice of me, considering she never gives us anything!"

"What?"

"Well, first she mentioned that I also gave her a jade pin for Christmas. And then she said," and Catherine's pleasing, low-pitched, rather husky voice became shriller and affected, mimicking Mary Stratton perfectly. 'You must like jade, dear.' When I said that I thought she did, she said, 'Not particularly,' and tossed it aside!"

Bill had to smile at Catherine's perfect imitation of his sister-in-law. "That's Mary, all right." He really couldn't see what Ed had ever seen in that woman. But something good had come out of that union. He did like young Michael. "Too bad you can't invite Michael. That was a great letter we got today from him, wasn't it? Thank God his injury wasn't worse. This might even mean he can come home, you know."

"I know, and Catherine softened. "Oh, I'll invite Mary. What the heyyy! It will be a big party—we won't have to see much of her!"

Bill laughed, even-tempered once again. "Great. And we'll put her up at the Waldorf. She likes it there. We'll tell her it would be too hectic here. It really will be, with Nancy, Carol, and Julie and their respective loafers."

And they smiled at each other.

CHAPTER 14

She locked the X-ray room securely and put the key in her pocket. Long ago she had borrowed the key from the technician and had a copy made. There wasn't much chance of anyone coming in at this time of night, but she didn't want to take the risk.

"I'm glad you put the key in your pocket," Michael said in a half-whisper from his wheelchair. "But I trust that pocket is going along with the dress—and everything else. Off." He had hastily stuffed half a dozen condoms in his bathrobe pocket before they left—though his expectations were a bit high. Now he surreptitiously slipped them out of his pocket and slipped two of them under his watchband.

Rita didn't notice his movements. She was completely engrossed in the sensations of her own body. "This won't be as comfortable as a bed, Michael." She smiled seductively, her soft Texas drawl more pronounced than usual. She took the light blanket from over his legs and threw it on top of the cold and narrow X-ray table. It looked great to Michael. But then, the floor would've looked great to him right then.

Michael had become friends with Rita during the long weeks of inaction. He had been pleasantly surprised at her intelligence, her education, the fact that she had obviously certain cultural advantages—and he was increasingly impressed with her sexual appeal. She exuded sex.

Rita began to take her clothes off—slowly. She threw the prim nurse's uniform carelessly on a stool, followed by her proper white slip. Standing there with her black garter belt, white stockings, lacy black panties, and a wisp of a sheer black brassiere, she vigorously shook her black curls, as if to get the hair out of her eyes, smiling at Michael all the while.

He was staring at her, hypnotized. She obviously didn't wear the Navy-issued skivvies. This was not underwear. It was definitely lingerie. He couldn't wait. Even as she reached down to remove her shoes, he caught her to him so that she half sat, half lay on his lap, cast and all, and passionately began kissing her face, her throat, her breast.

She responded immediately with feverish intensity, tearing off her remaining clothes and his, and somehow, with her surprisingly strong and able help, he was out of the wheelchair and lying on the table with her pretty face above his.

She realized soon enough that he was remarkably inexperienced, and the thought that she was initiating him into the mystery of love deepened her desire for him. She taught him much that first time. The world outside no longer existed for him. He was lost in sensations, lost in the woman above him. Even the fact that his control was not all it should be didn't diminish his deep pleasure.

It was over all too soon. After resting a moment, Michael, in mock horror, glanced up at the cumbersome X-ray machine hanging above them. "Heavy, heavy hangs over our heads," he murmured. "All three of them."

She looked at him questioningly. "It won't fall, Michael."

He laughed. "I know. I was just trying to make a joke. A little joke. Very little, now."

She obviously had bigger things on her mind, and he, too, again forgot everything but the woman so wonderfully active on top of him.

As, more slowly, they made love again, Michael was in more control. Afterwards they spent what seemed like an endless moment looking each other's eyes. He tried again to make a joke. "This would be a very different sort of picture, wouldn't it?"

"No, no, Michael, this machine is for taking pictures inside the body."

"Well, we weren't outside that long, were we?" Rita launched into a long technical explanation of the X-ray, and he gave up. He did miss Ruth.

* * *

The next morning he was quietly and happily remembering, lying back in his clean hospital bed, when Pete came in. He was delighted to see his friend, who had come over, as usual, on the shuttle bus from the Navy Receiving Station, but he didn't want to confide in him about Rita. He wanted to keep the secret knowledge hugged to himself, partly because of the very private sensuous memories, and partly because he was confused about his feelings towards both Ruth and Rita. He had to sort himself out first.

"You look satisfied. What do you know that I don't?" Pete asked.

Michael just laughed. Just then Rita swept in, and both men followed her with their eyes.

"That is some babe," Pete whistled appreciatively. "Hey, nurse! I feel pretty sick. How about kissing me and making me all better, huh?"

Rita laughed, but she looked around to make sure no other officer heard. She wasn't used to such brash behavior from the enlisted men.

Michael laughed, too. To his own surprise, Michael felt proud of the reaction she aroused in Pete rather than any form of jealously. He felt a proprietary interest in the woman, as if he were showing her off. He mused about his feelings for Ruth in such a situation and discovered, to his shocked surprise, that he would be jealous of Ruth if she showed an interest in another man, or even if another man showed interest in her.

"It won't be so bad, my new assignment," Pete muttered, watching Rita as she attended to the tubes of the soldier in the corner.

"What are you talking about?" With effort, he swung his attention back to Pete.

"I've been reassigned here, old buddy. They like my cooking here—not like some people I know who shall remain nameless—and I've been permanently attached to the Receiving Station. Besides," he added rather sheepishly, "the regular cook was transferred somewhere else. Some admiral ate here and liked it, so he took the cook."

All traces of a smile were wiped from Michael's face. The two men looked at each other. They would miss each other terribly when Michael was eventually reassigned.

Rita swung by on her way out, and although Michael looked up in the hope of some special recognition in her eyes, she smiled at both men equally.

CHAPTER 15

She had stayed strong for her broken-hearted mother and father, and her sobbing brother and sister-in-law. Sally was trying to comfort Ruth, but her warm companionship was the only consolation she would offer. They had just returned from the memorial service at the Temple, and although Ruth had not broken down during the service, now that they were in Ruth's bedroom, away from the shocked, grieving relative and friends milling about the house, Ruth finally let go and now couldn't seem to stop crying.

"He—he was my favorite brother, Sally," Ruth sobbed. "I loved him best! I still do . . ."

"I know, I know." Sally sat by Ruth on the bed, pushing her hair from her stricken face and patting her shoulder helplessly.

"Of course I'm proud of all my brothers," she said, gasping for breath. She didn't want to be disloyal, even in her grief. "But—but Jerry . . ." She broke down again. "Oh, Sally, he was shot down over Germany. We'll never know where. We'll never know."

Sally hugged Ruth.

"He was a bomber pilot in England, you know." Sally just nodded. She knew Ruth's brother well.

"He was so brave! And we'll never find out, we'll never see his body—oh, Sally!"

Sally tried to console her friend. "But don't you believe that the body is just a shell, that his—his soul still lives?" This was so unexpected from Sally that Ruth raised her head to look at her. Sally was a skeptic and usually had good rational explanations for all of Ruth's mystical experiences.

"Yes, of course, of course," Ruth agreed slowly. "But I thought you didn't believe . . ."

"It isn't that I don't believe, Ruth," Sally explained. She was relieved that Ruth seemed a bit more in control. "I sort of believe, but I don't want to see the future before it happens. That Mrs. Kaminsky of yours is probably right—I don't think she'd be a fake since she really doesn't make any money out of it, but . . ."

Ruth interrupted her in turn. The two girls knew each other so well that occasionally they could finish each other's sentences—and did. "She doesn't. She loses money. She bakes me wonderful cakes and cookies whenever I go over there."

"Okay, okay." Sally dared to smile, winning a slight but genuine smile in return. "Anyway, I don't mind that you don't believe. It keeps things interesting." She and Ruth actual managed a giggle.

"You're so great, Sally. I know you don't even like to talk about it. You're so . . . practical, you know." Ruth patted her friend's arm affectionately. "I really appreciate all you've done. You've been . . . you've been . . ." and she threatened to break down again.

"It's no big deal!" Sally spoke rather sharply, and it pulled Ruth up again.

That was Sally's favorite expression, and Ruth tolerated it, sometimes with annoyance and sometimes with amusement. Sally hated to be thanked, and Ruth was very appreciative. Their friendship prospered despite that major difference, or perhaps because of it.

"You always say that! When you decided to go to the Hop House <u>and</u> the USO just for me . . ."

Sally interrupted. "That was fun for me—another neat place to go. No big deal." She laughed at herself. Sally had a quick wit and sharp intelligence to go with her great legs, and she was her own favorite target.

"And when you asked Michael's mother about him I was so worried—even though you didn't believe in my dream . . ."

Sally was annoyed now. "It was no big deal, Ruth." And Ruth knew enough to keep quiet on the subject.

"Anyway, Sal, you're right about the body being only a shell. I guess I'm not crying for Jerry—I'm crying for me and for my parents and the rest of my family and friends. We'll all miss him so. And he was only twenty-one. He hadn't voted yet! And, of course, it makes me realize the danger that Michael and my brother Harry are still in." Although Ruth was still understandably sad, she seemed to be over her uncontrollable sobbing, and the crying itself had eased her grief. "Come on, let's get back to the others."

Ruth started to rise, but Sally didn't move. She seemed uncertain whether to speak or not. "Uhh, Ruth," she began hesitantly.

"What is it? Something wrong?"

"No, no, not at all." Sally's voice became stronger. "I just wanted to tell you that Harry is doing fine in the South Pacific. That's all."

Ruth was puzzled. "We haven't heard from him in about a month, although he was doing fine then. How . . . ?" And then the light dawned on her. "Oh, are you, uh, corresponding with Harry?" Ruth had no idea that Harry and Sally were interested in each other. What a wonderful development.

"Yes, we write to each other," Sally responded

airily. “Anyway, I thought it might make you feel better to know that he’s fine.”

“When did you last hear from him?” Ruth asked innocently. Wouldn’t it be marvelous if Sally married Harry? Then she would really be her sister!

Sally gave her a sharp look, but she slowly responded. “Yesterday. So he’s all right.”

“Sally . . .” Ruth couldn’t wait any longer as she prepared to cross-examine her friend.

Sally forestalled her neatly. “It’s no big deal,” she concluded as both girls, now smiling, left the room.

CHAPTER 16

Life settled down to a routine again for Ruth and her family. After all, they weren't the only ones to have a gold star replace one of the blue ones in the window. And the war effort had to go on. It kept them busy.

Max Braunstein returned to work at the shipyards after only two days, determined to do what he could to make the war shorter for his remaining son in peril, his Harry. Thank God at least David was safely married with a family and, temporarily at least, not likely to be drafted and therefore out of danger.

Etta Braunstein was quieter. She scarcely spoke. Somehow life had to go on, and she grimly set her mind to it. Although she normally kept the house immaculate, now the scrubbings and moppings occupied her days so that she was exhausted by night. But she still couldn't sleep. Ruth and Max realized she was coping in her own way, so they didn't criticize her constant and incessant cleaning.

Ruth returned to the store after two days, too. If her father could do it, she could too, even though working at The White House couldn't exactly qualify as part of the war effort. Still, someone had to work there. She couldn't bring herself to attend the Hop House just yet. Even thought that was definitely part of the war effort, she used to have too good a time flirting with the servicemen there to reconcile that with her grief.

Her personal loss had emphasized the fragile mortality of her other brothers, and of Michael. And all those other boys. Her heart did ache for them. But

Harry and Michael—nothing could happen to them. Could it?

Her "dream" had apparently really saved Michael that time. They had both confirmed it in letters, noting the differential between their time zones. God was looking out for them both. Did they have some kind of guardian angel? She didn't know. Mrs. Kaminsky didn't say anything about that. She always asked for protection from God and then they relaxed completely and meditated before they "read" Ruth's graduation ring or, as Ruth become more proficient in psychometry, when she read Mrs. Kaminsky's wedding ring or Mr. Kaminsky's watch. Mrs. Kaminsky said that any message she got when she was completely relaxed and protected was God talking to her. When she prayed, she was speaking to God. But she had never heard anything about a guardian angel. Someone or Something had saved Michael. She didn't know what it was. All she knew now was that her brother was lost. She hadn't had a dream or any intuition that he was even in danger, although being a bomber pilot was danger enough.

She was at home after work, sipping some weak tea and helplessly watching her mother scrub the kitchen cabinets—Etta definitely didn't want any help—when Sally phoned her.

"Say, I'm at the Hop House, and we're a little short of hostesses behind the counter tonight. I told them that maybe you could come over and help."

Ruth glanced toward where her mother was now scrubbing the walls and sighed. She would like to get out of the house. Would it be so bad if she went? If they needed her—

She told Sally to hold on for a moment and

went to her mother, wanting and needing approval and direction. "Mama, they need more girls behind the counter at the Hospitality House." The very fact that she had used the proper name showed the formality of the question. "Would it be right for me to go?"

Etta looked at her as if she didn't understand the question. Ruth repeated herself, and Etta sat down weakly in the nearest chair. She suddenly realized that she had been grieving so much that she was actually neglecting the loved ones she had left. Etta brought her head up and looked directly at Ruth. "So, why shouldn't you? You have to help the war effort too, don't you? And life has to go on, doesn't it? Her strength came back as she took a deep breath and said with an effort, "And—have a good time if you can. Life goes on."

As Sally hung up the phone, satisfied that she had persuaded Ruth to join the world again, she had a moment of doubt and hoped fervently she was doing the right thing for her best friend. And they really did need more help.

After Ruth left, Etta broke down and wept. Then she washed her face and combed her hair. It was time for Max to come home from his shift.

* * *

Ruth found herself feeling better as she was forced to keep a pleasant smile on her face as she served doughnuts and coffee to the servicemen.

She was arranging the doughnuts on plates when a feminine voice asked her, "Could I have some coffee and doughnuts, please?" She looked up, expecting a WAVE or a WAC or, what was even more rare, a woman Marine, and found instead a shabbily dressed, very young-looking girl with an infant in her arms standing in front of her.

Surprised, she said quickly, "Of course," and handed them to her. "The baby's hungry," the young girl, who didn't look more than sixteen or seventeen, stated matter of factly. She was having trouble balancing the baby in one arm while trying to pick up the plate in the other.

Ruth had absolutely no experience with babies, but she knew instinctively that coffee and a doughnut were not good for them. "How about some cream? I don't have any milk, but . . ." she asked her unexpected "customer."

"No," the girl hesitated, then smiled at Ruth. "He should have something warm. Coffee will be fine."

"And a doughnut? For a baby?"

"Oh yes, he's very hungry," and the young girl smiled brightly at Ruth again.

Ruth couldn't help insisting. "I have some cream—wouldn't you . . ." The girl seemed about to cry, so Ruth closed her mouth firmly and then said, "Would you like some for yourself?"

"That would be nice, thank you." The girl looked helplessly at the two cups of coffee and two plates of doughnuts in front of her.

"I'll carry these for you. You carry the baby," Ruth offered. She briskly helped her to a table. She purposely made it in two trips so that she could also carry a carton of cream to the table. Ruth noticed that the girl didn't even touch the cream as she began feeding the infant, holding the coffee cup to his lips and then alternating with a small piece of doughnut.

This was Ruth's first experience with real hunger or real ignorance—she wasn't quite sure which it was. She had a dollar and a half in her purse, but she sensed pride in the way the girl smiled so brightly, and she didn't want to insult her by offering money. At first she worried that a senior hostess would tell her to take her baby and leave, since she obviously wasn't in the Armed Forces, but everyone studiously ignored her. When Ruth came to her table later with refills of coffee and doughnuts, she appeared relieved and grateful that no fuss was being made, and Ruth sensed that she could do no more for her.

She was still puzzling over the young girl and her infant when she began to leave the Hop House with Sally. The girl had left long ago to disappear into the night as mysteriously as she had appeared. Although Sally had been in another section of the building at the time and hadn't seen her, she thought from Ruth's story that she was probably just hungry, although that was beyond Sally's experience as well. She didn't know why she didn't give the baby the cream. Homelessness and hunger were most common on the streets of San Francisco in 1942, but even so the two girls were having difficulty comprehending the situation.

It was just then that they ran into George Ward. Ruth had danced with George on numerous occasions over the past few months. He was quiet, tall, and rather slim, neither good looking nor bad looking, just kind of nondescript with his washed-out blonde hair and pale blue eyes. She had even gone to the movies with him twice; once to the Fox Theatre, with its elaborate red velvet interior to see Dana Andrews in The Purple Heart. Both of them had shed tears during the movie. He had never even tried to kiss her, which she thought was odd, but rather nice. All in all George seemed like a very pleasant, trustworthy young man. Somehow she felt a bit sorry for him, although she couldn't pinpoint just why.

George seemed genuinely glad to see her and insisted on seeing both girls onto the streetcar, saying that he would be proud to be seen escorting two such pretty girls. Smiles lit up both Ruth's and Sally's faces. They did make a striking pair—the tall, slender, stunning brunette a perfect foil for the short, curvaceous striking redhead. Sally was a trifle miffed though she didn't show it. She had purposely refused an invitation from a very handsome sailor to see <u>her</u> home so that she could be with Ruth. She shrugged to herself, "No big deal." She traded wisecracks with George, who turned out to be a bit of a wit, which surprised Ruth. She had never seen that side of him.

After Sally got off at her stop, he continued riding with Ruth and saw her to the house. She saw no harm in inviting him in, and he seemed glad of the invitation. Ruth set about making them some Postum. After a bit of small talk, she began telling him about the young girl she had met that evening. George seemed very interested and Ruth felt encouraged to open up a bit to him.

"I just didn't understand why she wouldn't give the baby some cream," she mused.

George's reaction surprised her even further.

"Could be that the baby was allergic to cream. My little brother had that problem and anything from a cow made him really sick."

"I've never heard of that," Ruth responded. "Do you have any other brothers or sisters? You've never told me about your family."

George paused for a moment. He seemed shaken. "I did have a family," he said slowly. "But they were lost in a terrible accident. About a year ago."

Ruth stopped what she was doing immediately and went to him. She put her hand on his shoulder and looked him in the eyes.

"Oh, George! I am so sorry! Can you tell me what happened?"

"It was a fire . . . it burned our house down to the ground . . . there was nothing they could do." He put his hand on hers. "If only I'd been there. I might have saved them!" His eyes were glistening with tears and Ruth didn't know what to do.

"Oh, George. It's so awful. You must be devastated."

At that, George pulled Ruth gently towards him and she slid onto his lap. She automatically wrapped her arms around him to comfort him and he responded by squeezing her tightly to him as his tears flowed freely.

"I'm all alone now," he sobbed. "All alone!"

This made Ruth begin crying, too, in part for George, but in great measure for the loss of her brother, Jerry.

"I lost my brother last month," she cried. "Jerry was my favorite and now he's gone." George held her more tightly and then, sweetly, innocently, he began kissing her forehead and her cheeks. When their lips finally met, they embraced with a fierce passion that shocked Ruth. She pulled away, gently, so as not to offend him.

"Let me get us something to wipe our faces with," she said hastily and got up from George's lap to find some napkins.

The two sat there silently enveloped in their grief for some time until George, finishing up his now-cold Postum, got up and said. “I’m going to go, Ruth. You’ve been swell. Thanks for the Postum and . . . for everything.”

As she waved goodbye to him from the front door, Ruth was both relieved and confused. The feeling she had for George had escalated so quickly. Did that mean that her love for Michael was waning? Was Michael going through the same thing?

It was then that she noticed the letter on the table. She tore open the V-Mail, noticing the signature first. It was Michael’s and above it was the word “love,” the first time he had written that. Her heart was beating so hard that she could hardly read his firm, strong handwriting. Then she sank down on the first chair she found. He had been awarded a Purple Heart, he was being sent home on a hospital ship, and he had asked her to marry him.

CHAPTER 17

"My boy, my boy!" Bridget wept a few happy tears at the good news that Michael was coming home, bad leg and all, home and out of that fearful danger, the saints be praised. Speaking of which, she took a bit of pleasure, surely, that the old lady had already left for New York for her brother-in-law's anniversary party before the mail had arrived. Bridget enjoyed being the first to know, as why shouldn't she be? Especially since he mentioned marrying that Ruth Braunstein confidential-like to Bridget. Michael had cautioned Bridget not to tell the old lady about the marriage plans just yet, as if she would! The old lady would have a temper tantrum, wouldn't she now, when she found out. A very well-bred temper tantrum, but a tantrum, no doubt.

Bridget had her own doubts about the marriage. Why not some of those sweet girls he had met in high school? Bridget was a snob in her own way. But if her boy loved this Ruth and wanted to marry her, then he should have her.

Michael had written, "if Ruth will have me." Hah! What right-minded lass wouldn't have her fine, upstanding young lad! She'd jump at the chance, surely.

His poor leg must be getting better, certainly, the saints be praised. She would go to Mass directly to give her heartfelt thanks. And Bridget went about her dusting with a smile transforming the wrinkles on her face and tears of happiness in her expressive brown eyes.

CHAPTER 18

Mary Stratton was not in a good mood after traveling for three days, first on The City of San Francisco, and then transferring in Chicago to The Broadway Limited to New York. She had almost been bumped by some soldiers, but at the last minute they found room for her, although it was not what <u>she</u> would call room. The mass of people going from one place to another was horrendous. She realized that the war effort required the train to carry the military first, of course, but did they have to be so—so boisterous, so <u>low-class</u>? And, though she hated to admit it, some were even odorous. Couldn't they at least bathe? <u>She</u> had managed a somewhat unsatisfactory sponge bath every morning.

The roomettes she had engaged were adequate enough, though very tiny, of course, and she had to admit that the dining service and the food were satisfactory on both trains. She had actually enjoyed her first breakfast, when she had ordered ham and eggs for forty-five cents and a pot of real coffee for another twenty cents. She was relieved, however, when the train finally clanged to a stop at Penn Central. Detraining with her matched luggage, she hailed an already-overburdened porter. Tall, elegant and seemingly untouched by the chaos around her, she stood and waited for her brother-in-law to find her.

She stood for ten long minutes. Finally, she heard Catherine's voice before she saw her sister-in-law trying to break through the crowd toward her. Why in the world didn't the woman bring her chauffeur to help her—or why didn't William come himself?

Catherine, breathless, finally reached her. "Lucky I phoned and found out the train was going to be late. How are you, Mary? It's been a long time." Both women pressed their cheeks together in a pale imitation of an embrace. Not long enough, Mary thought, as she eyed Catherine somewhat coldly.

"Forgive me, my dear," Mary said crisply, "but I had a most miserable trip here. You just wouldn't believe the substandard conditions I had to endure. One little suggestion, though—if you called and knew the time I was coming in, then why . . . " and she paused delicately.

"It's crowded out there, Mary. It's very difficult for anyone to get through. I started in plenty of time, but I really couldn't help being a little late."

"Perhaps if you had brought William—or your chauffeur—" Again, the suggestion was intimated.

"It's hard enough for one person, Mary. Both Bill and Roscoe are busy. Bill is working and Roscoe is running errands for the party. Oh, come on, Mary, let's get out of this." Catherine looked, dismayed, at Mary's luggage. The porter had long since disappeared, immediately after Catherine had given him the magnanimous tip of twenty-five cents per bag. "You haven't engaged a Red Cap yet?"

"I was waiting here, dear."

"Mmm, yes. Well, stay here, Mary. I'll go get a Red Cap." Anything, Mary thought, to get away from the woman.

Fifteen minutes later, Catherine, now in not much better a mood than Mary, returned with a thin, elderly black man in tow. "I actually had to fight for him," she puffed. The Red Cap looked overwhelmed by the three pieces of luggage. Catherine, wondering why anyone would bring so much luggage for one weekend, picked up the overnight case herself.

Mary's look said it all. To demean herself in this way! Her sister-in-law wasn't a stevedore, for heaven's sake.

"I was lucky enough to get a parking space near-by. Come along, Mary," and Catherine ran interference for both the frail looking overloaded Red Cap and Mary.

When they reached the car, she tipped the elder-ly man generously, giving him a dollar bill, while Mary seated herself in the car, waiting. The Red Cap looked as if he were about to faint, but Catherine couldn't tell if it was from the exertion or her abundant tip. She was relieved when he tottered off smiling and nodding, expressing his voluble thanks, apparently as well as could be expected.

As Catherine pulled out into traffic, she asked brightly, "How have you been?"

"Just fine, dear—except for this terrible trip, of course. But I wouldn't miss your anniversary, dear. By the way, I inadvertently left your gift at home—on my dresser, all wrapped, in fact. I will mail it when I return."

Catherine nodded. "Thank you, Mary." She thought, ironically, that if all the gifts Mary had "left on her dresser, all wrapped" were piled on top of one another, the roof would be punctured. When Mary actually gave a gift, it was the topic of conversation for months.

"I'm driving you to the Waldorf, Mary. As I wrote, things are just too hectic with the girls and their husbands staying at the house, and I know you like peace and quiet. You always like it at the Waldorf."

"That will be fine, dear. What time will you call for me for the party?"

"I'll have Roscoe pick you up at 7:30. It will be a formal, sit-down dinner, of course, and we'll serve at 8:00. That will be plenty of time for you to arrive." And not too much of you before we all go into dinner, Catherine noted. Anyone else would have walked the few blocks, especially in view of gas rationing. Mary was just lucky that Catherine hadn't been using the car too much lately so that there was sufficient gas in the huge black Packard, which couldn't seem to pass a gas station without stopping to guzzle up the rations.

Although Mary had inexplicably accepted the change of accommodation without protest, she was most displeased that the chauffeur would call for her instead of a member of the family. She remained silent for the rest of the journey, despite Catherine's weakening attempts at conversation. How rude of Catherine, Mary fumed, having the hired help do the job the family should do. How terribly lax and ill bred.

As she pulled in front of the Waldorf, Catherine attempted to be a bit more cordial. "Everything is all set for you, Mary. We have arranged everything, including sending the bill to us, of course. All you have to do is report to the front desk." Mary did manage to thank her—but of course, that arrangement was the least Catherine should do. And then she was discourteous enough to not even leave her car to see her into the hotel, but shot off like a bullet as soon as the bellboys had removed her luggage.

Catherine recalled, as she sped off, that she hadn't even mentioned Michael's letter. Well, Mary no doubt received one, too. That in itself should have been enough to put her in a good mood. Then again,

Catherine had never seen her in a really good mood. 'Good' was a relative term, of course, especially when it came to Mary.

Mary, a bit mollified after being shown to one of the better suites, decided she was going to do something for herself for a change and spent the rest of the day shopping, napping, bathing and primping for the party, in that order. She had decided on her new gray long suit, which swept the floor, with the smart matching jacket. Too bad it wasn't silk, but the material was similar—it certainly had cost enough. She knew she looked elegant, and she was satisfied. Then she sat and waited for the chauffeur. She didn't care for—what was his name—Roscoe, at all. She found him very familiar and insolent. He obviously had never been taught what his proper place and station were.

If anything, Roscoe, naturally gregarious and friendly and treated by Catherine and Bill as one of the family, disliked the short drive back to the Park Avenue brownstone even more than Mary did.

Mary wanted to make a grand entrance in her new suit, but unfortunately for Roscoe, they were stuck in traffic for a good twenty minutes, so they were a little late, and everyone was just going in to dinner when she arrived. She was hardly noticed in the crowd of one hundred and twenty-five guests all headed for the main ballroom, where the seven-course dinner, accompanied by a variety of wines, was to be served. After hurriedly dropping her coat with the butler (he looked new—probably hired for the occasion, she thought contemptuously), she found herself alongside a middle-aged couple who looked vaguely familiar.

"I'm Mary Stratton, William's sister-in-law," she offered, extending her hand. They stopped in mid-stride. "I hate to have to introduce myself, but I do suppose Catherine has other things to do. I haven't seen her yet. Nobody met me at the door but the butler." She managed a world of reproach with her opening statement.

"Eduardo and Carmelita Sabrella," the tall, elegant gentleman replied, courteously shaking her hand, while his beautiful dark-eyed wife smiled graciously.

Now Mary knew where she had seen them before. They were the Sabrellas! She had seen their picture frequently in the society pages. How had Catherine ever snagged them?

"Eduardo—what a lovely name. My late husband's name was Edward, too, you know. Edward Stratton," she emphasized, hoping they had heard of him. There was no reaction, so she bubbled chattily on. What was that she had read about their children? No, it was just a daughter. Oh yes, she had joined the Army or Navy or something. "How is your daughter? I read about her patriotic endeavor in the newspaper. So unselfish of her."

Their faces became bland. "Fine, just fine," they murmured, almost in unison.

"Where is she stationed now?" Mary was oblivious to the reserve inherent in both the Sabrellas. "I can't remember exactly—," she paused. The pause lengthened. Both Eduardo and Carmelita had seen the article in the newspaper, and both hated it.

Carmelita graciously broken the silence. "Yes, our daughter, Rita, is a Navy nurse stationed in New Caledonia. Thank you for asking." Her tone, in its charmingly accented English, though courteous in the extreme, had a finality about it that would have silenced even Mary if the coincidence had not struck Michael's mother so forcibly.

"My son is in the Navy hospital in New Caledonia," she responded. "Near a place called Noumea."

That commanded the full attention of both Carmelita and Eduardo, as they looked at each other and then sharply at her.

"Amazing," Eduardo murmured, half under his breath. He had just a trace of a Spanish accent.

Mary was all smiles. "Perhaps they know each other! Wouldn't that be a coincidence? Perhaps your daughter Rita is taking care of my son Michael. His leg was hurt in a battle on the Lexington. Why, she could be bringing him his meals, helping him to—" and her voice trailed off when she finally realized their reaction.

Eduardo and Carmelita had become positively grim. Was it not bad enough that their wonderful, beautiful, talented only daughter should be as a servant to others such as the son of this terrible woman? That she should actually list those onerous duties that they tried to forget was unforgiveable.

Eduardo bowed to Mary with cold finality. "Excuse us, please, Mrs. Stratton. We must go in to dine." And, taking a shocked Carmelita by the arm, steered her to their assigned seats in the ballroom.

Mary watched them depart with a gleam in her eye. Now, why couldn't Michael cultivate someone like that? She would definitely suggest in her next letter that, if he didn't already know Rita Sabrella, that he should look her up. He could certainly mention that his mother had met her parents recently at a party in his uncle's home, and she went over the letter in her mind, finding just the correct words to push him properly in the right direction. She sighed. He was stubborn so often. It was important that he not be stubborn in this particular instance.

Catherine, stunning in a white off-the-shoulder gown with a touch of gold, caught sight of the Sabrellas seating themselves and smiled to herself. Although the Roosevelts, the Vanderbilts, and the Kennedys had sent their regrets, the Sabrellas had accepted, and she thoroughly enjoyed the muted excitement their presence caused. She noted with concern, however, that they looked somewhat disturbed, and she made her way to them to see if she could help them in any way, chatting with her other guests as she went. Suddenly she caught sight of Mary, standing statuesquely at the entrance to the ballroom, obviously waiting for something or someone. She sighed. She hadn't greeted her yet. That's what Mary was waiting for. She had better rectify that oversight. Mary was capable of spoiling her entire party.

"Mary! How nice to see you. You look lovely." At least the statement was true, she thought generously.

"Thank you, dear. What a beautiful gown, Catherine. You don't think it's too young for you?"

Mary wondered why Catherine actually laughed.

"Probably so, Mary," she agreed amiably, thinking the woman had to be heard to be believed. "But to keep young, one must feel young, right?"

"Well . . ." Mary was taken aback by this strange reaction to her statement. She had been honestly offering a helpful suggestion. She was always strictly honest, even when it hurt (especially then, because then the individual needed it most), and the gown was in very poor taste for a woman of Catherine's years.

Catherine changed the subject. "We heard from Michael yesterday. Isn't it wonderful?"

"You have? I haven't—not for at least a week or so. What is wonderful?" Mary was at full alert.

"Why, his news, Mary. He is being sent home. Really sent home! And he was awarded a Purple Heart. The mail must have missed you while you were traveling."

"Of course. Naturally, he would have told me first." Mary was at a disadvantage having to hear the news from Catherine, but she was glad he was coming home. She did suffer a slight twinge of regret having to rule out the Sabrella possibility. "He deserves a Purple Heart. That will come in handy later in life, too. How is his leg?"

"Getting along fine." Catherine was genuinely happy for the happiness she bestowed—but it didn't last long.

As if she were ashamed of her momentary lapse into maternal love, Mary covered up with a rather sharp, self-satisfied question that she must have known would devastate Catherine. "And how are your sons-in-law? Since they are either over draft age or foreigners, they certainly don't have to worry about getting into the war. Any of them found a position yet?"

Catherine would have given a great deal if she could have answered airily in the affirmative, but she didn't do so badly. "I am so fortunate in having three fine sons-in-law," she answered softly. "They are wonderful husbands for the girls. And there's love there. For Kay and Nicky, Victoria and Lee, and Nancy and

Anatoly, there is love there—and that is the main thing." They both were silent for a moment as Mary girded up to sink the knife in deeper, but Catherine forestalled her. "Oh, to answer your question," as if she had forgotten, "They've all had offers and are considering them. Imagine that! Aren't they lucky? I've got to get back now to my other guests. You know where you sit, of course. See you later." And Catherine escaped with a half-lie that could never be proven, yea or nay. Mary had her suspicions, but put that on file as she made her entrance into the party.

And Catherine slowly realized, as she walked toward the Sabrellas, that she had stumbled on the truth when she had told Mary about the love that enveloped each couple. That was the main, thing, wasn't it?

CHAPTER 19

Pete was desolate. He was exalted, excited. But he was desolate. He wandered along the peaceful sandy beach, kicking a shell here and there, but he achieved no peace. How the hell was he to know the broad was Mike's? Sure, he set out with the express intention of making time with her, once he saw her in the hospital. Who wouldn't? Then, when he saw her walking alone by the beach, sure he made his move. All systems were go for him with that lady—and he knew it. It only took two dates, and when he took her to that great little French inn further inland, they literally flew at each other. He narrowed his eyes as he recalled their fierce lovemaking—they were almost fighting, but they were fighting to unite, not to separate. He had no control over the inevitable arousal that came with the memory.

He wouldn't have made time with Michael's lady—but he didn't know. He didn't know. Christ! He didn't even see Mike those couple of days—he was too busy with the broad.

He strolled by the dock where nickel was loaded and unloaded and almost bumped into a soldier at the end of a block-long line of servicemen waiting to enter The Pink House. He excused himself and went on his solitary way. It had been awhile since he had availed himself of the available ladies at The Pink House, he mused. This was a long line even considering the lack of available women in New Caledonia, but then he remembered it was payday. The lines were always longer on payday.

What made the whole mess worse, what made it so much worse was Rita's goddamned fucking honesty. That was a good one. Her goddamned fucking honesty about fucking. Why the hell did she have to tell him about Mike afterwards? If she had to tell him, why didn't she tell him before they went to bed? Or keep her fucking mouth shut? That was a good one, too—and the memories flooded him again.

And the, and then—he moaned with the injustice of it all. She actually had to tell Mike. Mike! She had explained it very carefully to Pete. Some shit about her code of honor. Honor! This was his and Mike's friendship being threatened. She had explained to Pete that, although she felt herself a "free spirit," as she had quaintly put it, she did not dispense her favors indiscriminately. She liked Mike and she liked Pete, and she wasn't going to "bed," as she put it, both of them at the same period of time, because she didn't feel right about it, even though she had "bedded" Mike quite often over the past few weeks. What was more, she wasn't ashamed of what she did any more than he was, although the affair had to be kept secret, of course, because of that silly rule which prohibited an officer from fraternizing with an enlisted man, and she wanted to be "above board and honorable" about the whole thing. Shit! He was afraid to face Michael. And he couldn't blame Mike for getting mad. Christ! He sure would, in Mike's place.

And what made it unbearably unendurable was the fact that Rita and he really went for each other. He had feelings toward her and her expert lovemaking that he had never had for another—and she had told him she wasn't going to bed Mike again, now that she had met him, because she had feelings for him that she didn't have for Mike. He had always considered himself a ladies' man and an expert lover himself. He made love to please the broads, which pleased him. But this one! Fire and lightning together they were, until they were both sated.

He really liked Rita, too. He even confided in her his completely impossible ambition to be a doctor, something he had only told Mike, and their mutual interest in medicine drew Pete and Rita even closer together.

And, though he hated to admit it, he admired her crazy "code of honor." He respected her honestly. He seemed to be falling for the dame. What the hell was he going to do?

CHAPTER 20

Michael sat in his wheelchair, cradling the cup of hot, strong coffee in both his hands as if he were cold, looking out of the window at the crashing waves. Everything had happened too fast. He was still confused about exactly what he should be feeling, about exactly what he was feeling. But on one point he was crystal-clear in his thinking. Ruth was the one for him. No one else. Somehow he had always loved her, even when he was making love to Rita. Somehow it was all a preparation for Ruth, as crazy as that seemed. And somehow she would be able to love him, physically love him as he knew she wanted to. She had to.

He had received her letter an hour ago. It lay on his lap so that he could re-read it, feel it on his body. The V-Mail that opened with shaking, nervous fingers showed just one word—a huge "YES," so big it was hardly legible. At the bottom she signed, "Love, Ruth" primly, but her exuberance showed in the decorations on the sides—X's and O's, for kisses and hugs, alternated all around the page. Funny, the necking he had with Ruth had been more thrilling in its way than the real thing with Rita—or was that sour grapes? The real thing had been great, no denying that.

What he wasn't sure about was his reaction to Rita's news flash. She had out-Winchelled Walter Winchell with his news to everyone and to "all the ships at sea." He really wasn't jealous of Pete, strange as that seemed to him. He even tried to be jealous, thinking that was the proper reaction, but it was phony, he had to face that. Maybe he wasn't normal.

Well, whatever he was, he wasn't going to be what he wasn't. So he wasn't jealous.

Actually, he was a bit relieved. Though God knows why.

He appreciated Ruth more, that was for sure. And what did he feel for Rita? Affection. A bit of a bruised ego, sure. But affection remained. The lady was great. Unbelievably honest.

What about his mother? He shuddered. Well, he had his own life to live, didn't he? At least he hoped he had. He was lucky to get away with a sore leg, and he knew it. The doctor shot him with something new called Penicillin that was supposed to take care of any infection, and he did feel better now.

And Pete? He couldn't blame Pete. Where was Pete? He wanted to see him, to tell him they were still good buddies—but where was he? He would be leaving soon to go home, and he hadn't even told Pete that he was being sent home to the States. And Pete would stay here. He didn't want to leave without talking to him. He'd phoned and phoned, but Pete never returned the call. How could he tell him he understood if he couldn't talk to him?

CHAPTER 21

Madeline Kaminsky's face was as impassive as she could make it, and she handed back the small silver ring to Ruth. "I'm sorry, hon. I just couldn't read anything this time. Nothing came through." Her voice sounded hollow in her own ears, and she didn't dare look at her husband.

Ruth turned the ring over in her hand for several seconds herself before slipping it back on her finger. It had been her high school graduation gift, and she treasured it. There was no stone, but the engraving on the shiny surface was intricate, in the form of tiny knots, and the engraving within simply said, "Love from Mom & Dad," which took up all the space inside to that "Dad" was right up against "Love."

Ruth was not only deliriously happy about Michael's completely unexpected proposal of marriage, but she was full of wonder and awe at what had happened during her meditation today. She had actually received a thrilling message that she did have a guardian angel who was looking after her. She had often wondered about that, and when she found out, it again was if she had always known it.

Although for a moment it seemed to Mrs. Kaminsky that Ruth looked suspiciously at her friend, the moment passed, and Ruth, too happy to think otherwise, believed what she wanted to believe. "Well, I know we can't always read, but it is a bit of a disappointment—especially now."

Ruth wanted so terribly to be reassured about her future, that Michael's leg would heal and he would be healthy and whole, which was the main thing, and that she and Michael would be happy ever after. She hoped fervently that Mrs. Kaminsky was right, that the doctors were wrong and that she could make love. At one of her first readings in what was called psychometry, Mrs. K. had thrilled her by knowing about her illness, about the doctors' warnings, about her own fear that she couldn't consummate a real marriage. And she had told her that she could see no problem there, that the doctors were wrong. Of course, she also warned her that even the best psychometrists were only 80% correct. Mrs. K. had added drily that she just hoped she wasn't 80% wrong.

Mrs. K. had gone through the same ritual, the exact ritual that she had taught Ruth so that she could do what Mr. K. called a "reciprocal trade agreement." Ruth couldn't do very much yet, although Mrs. K assured her, that, with practice, she would get better and didn't stint her at all with her own readings. She would always relax all of them first from their feet to the top of their heads in a comfortable chair (not too comfortable—once Ruth had actually gone to sleep, which had struck them all as so funny that they giggled helplessly through the whole evening and couldn't meditate at all), and then she would call on God to protect them. Ruth discovered that, although Mr. and Mrs. K. believed devoutly in God, they really didn't believe in organized religion. They believed God was inside everyone and everything, and with belief in God one could do anything. They believed God wanted the best for everyone, but that people sometimes put obstacles in their own way by worrying needlessly and having the wrong attitude. They believed that, if you prepared for the best and knew the best was coming to you, the best would come to you.

After Mrs. K. had made sure that none of them had their legs or arms crossed, which she said cut off the vibrations (once Ruth crossed her eyes, and again they all collapsed into laughter), she closed her eyes and put what she called "the white light of God's protection" about them by visualizing it, calling upon God to protect them and saying, "Naught but good can enter here," all of which caused goose bumps to raise on Ruth's uncrossed arms. Then, after a short period of meditation for all of them, she took Ruth's ring and turned it slowly in her left hand, asking God for the power to read it. She said that whatever came to her mind then, and she was surprisingly accurate. Mr. K. sometimes handled the ritual, but he was a reticent, somewhat reserved gentleman who preferred his wife to lead them.

But Madeline Kaminsky couldn't reassure Ruth this time. She had read danger for Ruth ahead, and she knew she mustn't sow that tainted seed in her little friend's mind. She could be wrong—sometimes she was—and just that seed itself could cause the very trouble it was supposed to foretell. Besides, Ruth was stronger than she realized. She would survive her troubles if troubles there were, and it could do no good to tell her of them. Mrs. Kaminsky hated to censor what was right to tell and what wasn't, but in this case she knew it was necessary. At least Ruth now knew she had a guardian angel to protect her—she had been so happy when she told the Kaminskys.

"How about some tea and brownies?" Mrs. Kaminsky smiled. "I made some with nuts especially for you."

That was the one problem with Mrs. K. Ruth was always trying to diet, and the older woman was always making something great just for her, so that Ruth would be rude if she refused and fat if she didn't. And it was always something Ruth loved, which made it more difficult. Ruth just didn't know how to solve the problem without hurting the older woman's feelings—and that just wouldn't do.

"Just a very small piece, Mrs. K., please. I am trying to diet, you know, but I can't resist your goodies," Ruth hinted as broadly as she could.

Mrs. Kaminsky's intuition didn't seem to extend to her misguided generosity. She beamed at Ruth, taking the surrender of her diet as a tribute to her own good baking. Mr. Kaminsky, a roly-poly elf of a man, was already choosing his second brownie with obvious relish.

Ruth sighed and enjoyed the brownie. "What I really dread now is going to see his mother."

"You won't have to do that until he comes home. I doubt that he's even told her yet. He'll probably do that when he gets her, don't you think?"

"You think he hasn't told her yet?" Ruth looked up at her friend.

Mrs. Kaminsky shook her head and laughed. "Ruth, I really don't know. I don't know everything. Even when I read the jewelry, I'm sometimes wrong. But, knowing how formidable Mrs. Stratton is, I would think that even Michael might be a bit afraid of her. There's been no father there for years, and he is an only child. She would likely be a problem for him no matter who he decided to marry."

"You're probably right." Even my parents aren't overjoyed." Ruth resisted another brownie and finished her tea. "They're so orthodox, you know, and Michael isn't Jewish, of course. I can imagine how his mother feels. They're even society people. And she never liked me. Even before I met Michael." Ruth smiled, but the sparkle in her expressive green eyes was somewhat shadowed by the seemingly insurmountable obstacle that lay ahead.

"Your strong enough to stand up to her, Ruth." Mrs. Kaminsky spoke reassuringly. "You can do it. Just think of Michael, how much you love him. After all, she is his mother. If it weren't for her, he wouldn't be here. You can be grateful to her for that, can't you?"

"What a wonderful way of looking at it, Mrs. K.," Ruth was comforted for the moment, reflecting on that simple fact.

"How are your own parents taking it?"

"It's not easy. My mother is crying most of the time, and my father looks so sad. I don't know what I'd do without Sally. She's been great." Ruth brushed her long shining red hair from her face. "I know they're only afraid for me, that I'll be hurt. It's just that they love me, of course." Ruth had a sudden flash of the truth. "And I'm just afraid for them. I don't want to hurt them. I know they would have preferred me to marry into my own religion. What a silly circle!"

"But a nice one," Mrs. Kaminsky smiled. "Love will keep you all together." *No matter what*, she thought. *No matter what.*

As she saw Ruth to the door, she looked up and down the street to make sure all the blinds were down to prevent any light showing in the blackout. As air-raid warden for her block, she really should leave the house to investigate properly. She sighed and went for her coat, praying God would grant Michael as much love to give Ruth as she obviously had to offer him.

That might be Ruth's only salvation. The premonition of real danger, however, bothered her. She prayed for protection for her. That was all she could do.

CHAPTER 22

Pete couldn't even forget his problems as he watched the two big men pummel each other in the ring at the Triangle Gardens, much as he usually enjoyed watching the fights. He sipped his fourth strong Aussie beer, wishing it were the even stronger Butterfly Rum, which wasn't served here at the ringside tables. He had stood in line for fifteen minutes to pick up his four beers, which, at ten cents for each large paper cup, was a bargain, but it wasn't enough to dull his pain. He had finally stopped at the hospital to tell Mike that he had fallen in love with the broad and even wanted to marry her, although he hadn't asked her yet, but that he didn't know about Mike's prior claim when he made his move—and that he wouldn't have, had he known—only to find that Michael had been sent home.

The Triangle Gardens was nothing more or less than a huge beer garden in the shape of a triangle, surrounded by a seven-foot bamboo fence, and operated by the Navy for all the servicemen. The portable boxing ring provided free prizefights now and again, which Pete usually enjoyed thoroughly.

He watched dully as the soldier in the ring solidly landed a right cross to the sailor's jaw, and the sailor went down for the count. Just like Pete. And Mike, because of Pete. He glanced as his watch. He was to meet Rita in thirty minutes at the French inn just outside of Noumea, on the other side of the island from the hospital, and he didn't want to be late. Damn it, he did love her and she loved him, and he wasn't going to give her up, but he hated to sacrifice his best friend in the process.

He made his way through the hundreds of servicemen and the rare nurse or two at the tables, all with one or more paper cups full of beer in front of them, and all yelling heartily for the champion of their particular branch of service. As he neared the entrance, he found the usual families of Kanakas, the men dressed in jeans and khaki shirts, some with sweat bands around their bushy black hair, cut straight up the sides and sometimes colored red like the iron-rich earth, and the women in colorful missionary-type muu-muus, resting quietly outside in the beautiful park-like area. He also saw the occasional indentured Tonkinese or Javanese servant in their black pajama-like pants and jackets, with the conical, oriental hats with wide brims to shade their faces, hurrying to and fro. It had been found that the Melanesians, known to the servicemen as Kanakas, did not make good servants to the French in this French colony, since they were comfortable landowners and saw no need to work.

On his way to his jeep, he also noticed a Frenchman or two, dressed in tropical-weight slacks, and even an older Frenchwoman, smartly if quietly dressed in a light dress and sweater. The French children and young girls had all been sent to New Zealand when it was felt the island was in danger of occupation by the Japanese. The Battle of the Coral Sea that Michael and Pete had both so recently participated in had effectively stopped the invasion, but the younger French generation was now in New Zealand. Pete thought wryly that now that they had protected them from the Japanese, they were protecting them from the Americans.

He jumped into the jeep assigned to him, thanking the powers that be that he was a cook and so could sign out a jeep whenever necessary to pick up fruits, vegetables, or whatever they needed on this beautiful island. He must remember to pick up some fruit after he saw Rita.

Yes, this sub-tropical island, with its mountains and its banyan trees, was beautiful in the mild winter, despite the sparse tropical foliage here and there and despite the heavy winds and typhoons that sometimes ripped the roofs off the houses, the opposite of what it would be back home in California. The metal corrugated roofs were nailed down on some of the wooden structures that served as homes for the poorer Polynesians, although the stucco bungalows were actually quite nice. He caught a glimpse of a child taking a bath in a bucket-like contraption in the back of one of the more primitive houses.

Rita was waiting for him in their favorite curtained booth in the dining area when he arrived, though he was five minutes early. He joined her, both their faces lighting up as they greeted each other.

"Have you been waiting long?" He kissed her lightly on the cheek, since it wasn't private enough to dare more between an officer and an enlisted man, as the curtains didn't close all the way, but the simple kiss thrilled both of them with the promise of what was to come.

"Not really," Rita purred. "I got off a little early, and I was anxious to see you—more anxious than usual," she laughed, as she saw his reaction. "I have something for you." Then she laughed again. "Not that, Pete, not that! Well, besides that! I have a letter for you."

Had Pete known of Michael's disappointment with Rita's sense of humor, he would have disagreed whole-heartedly. He loved her sense of humor.

"A letter? Who from, baby?" He wasn't really paying attention to her words as his hand caressed hers lovingly.

"From Michael, Pete," and Rita had Pete's full attention.

"Mike?" Pete was astounded and not a little wary. "How? Why?"

"He gave it to me to give to you, Pete. He said it was important, although, of course, I have no idea what it says." Rita handed him the envelope without any hesitation.

Pete thought bemusedly that Rita was the only dame in the world that wouldn't steam open a letter like this out of curiosity. It was actually very handy to have a broad with a code of honor.

"Go ahead, open it now, Pete," Rita said softly. "I know you're anxious."

"Well, okay," he replied hesitantly, not knowing what he would find. He steeled himself and tore open the envelope. His smile began in the first paragraph, and by the end of the letter he was laughing with pleasure and deep relief. "He's okay, baby, he's okay!"

"I told you everything was fine," Rita agreed.

"He's going to marry his girl at home, and he understands about us, baby! He understands about us. I'll write him tomorrow." His tone changed to one of concern. "I sure hope he's not marrying on the re-bound, though."

"Oh, I don't think so, darlin'" Rita was amused. "At least he knows what to do now!"

Pete roared with laughter. He loved this lady. He wouldn't feel kindly toward any man who tried to make time with her now, but he didn't begrudge her the past, which was certainly more colorful than his own.

"I'll tell you, honey, this is the third time in my life I have been this relieved. The first time was when I was a kid, when I crawled under that big semi, then getting out of the Lady Lex whole and healthy, along with Mike, almost whole and healthy, and this time. I wouldn't have wanted to hurt Mike, baby, even for you."

"I know that, darlin'. But tell me, what was this business of crawling under a truck? That sounds just horrible."

"Oh, I was about six or seven, I guess. Just a little guy without too much sense. Bobby and I—Bobby was the kid next door—went over to Bayshore and Alemany where there was a great swamp to catch frogs. Well, the great white hunters flubbed, so we looked around for something else to do. There was this real steep hill, see, on the Bayshore going up to Silver Avenue, and the big trucks went up real slow—slow enough for a kid to latch on to them and hang on. We waited for a big one with a trailer, and Bobby jumped up on the inside and I got up on the outside. So, being not too bright, I decided that I wanted to be on the inside with Bobby instead. But, instead of going over the yoke connecting the truck to the trailer, I crawled underneath." Pete stopped and lit both his cigarette and Rita's. "I'll never forget those huge wheels slowly coming toward me as I scrambled through. Good thing I was fast!" He was laughing until he saw her face.

"You could have been killed!" She was horrified.

"Honey, honey, you know I'm all right now. Better than ever, believe me." He shook his head. "That was even worse than hanging on back of the street cars when they went by, though."

"What a naughty little boy you were—and you certainly started early," Rita scolded.

They both quieted as the elderly waitress came to take their orders. Rita had only ordered coffee. They both ordered steaks. They would need their strength.

When the waitress left, Pete cleared his throat. "Baby, you know how I feel about you," he began awkwardly. "I love you, kid."

"I know, Pete, darlin'." Rita spoke so softly he had to bend his head to hear her. "You know I love you, too." She didn't speak the words lightly. It was the first time she had ever uttered them to anyone outside her family.

Pete took her hand in both of his. His tone was gruff. "I never loved a dame before, Rita. This is the first time."

That did thrill her. "That is a coincidence, Pete, honey. It's the same way with me."

He looked at her and believed her. "We were meant for each other, kid. Let's get married."

That surprised her. But, as she thought about it, she realized that she did want to spend the rest of her life with this man. She dismissed the thought of her parents' probable objections as easily as she dismissed the thought of the probable court-martial if the Navy found out about it. This would have to be carefully orchestrated, though. But everything could be worked out in time.

"Yes, Pete, let's," Rita agreed. And it was settled.

* * *

It was much later, up in "their" room, which the understanding landlady always managed to give them, that they began to work out the details. They were relaxing after their strenuous lovemaking, both lying naked and content on the bed under the mosquito netting that was so necessary on the island, rolled up for the daytime, of course. Although there was no danger of malaria in New Caledonia, dengue fever was a real threat. All the men checked their mosquito netting for holes, keeping in mind the "Sad Sack" cartoons which showed a mosquito bombing down onto a large hole in the mosquito netting which framed its target, the bare backside of a sleeping serviceman.

"We'll have to wait until after the war, Pete. No sense getting in trouble with the Navy," Rita said sensibly. "We'll be together all we can meanwhile, of course." She smiled knowingly at him.

Pete had to agree. As far as they were concerned, they were engaged. Pete even determined to pick up a ring he had his eye on in Noumea for her. It didn't look like an engagement ring, it was just a little silver circlet engraved with tiny hearts, but that was all the better. Like she said, no sense getting in trouble.

He had already told her about his big family and of his own ambitions. Somehow he was going to work his way through college and become a doctor. They would have a good life together.

She had never told him of her family, though. And so he asked her. She laughed, but it had a hard edge to it. "My family is very different, Pete. My parents came from Spain, and they settled in Texas. They're great—don't misunderstand me—and they would do anything for me and I would do anything for them—but sometimes they don't understand at first. After I explain it to them, that's a different story."

Pete envisioned an impoverished immigrant family newly arrived from Spain and immediately offered to help. "I'm used to family, babe. A few more mouths to feed wouldn't hurt us at all. If you like, when we're married, we can bring them to San Francisco where we can take care of them better." He felt quite pleased with himself for such a magnanimous offer. It wasn't every Joe that would support his wife's family. And the thought that she would be his wife sent warmth and contentment right down to his toes.

Now Rita hesitated. "That's great of you, sweetheart, really great, and I do appreciate it. But there's really no need. My parents are quite—well, comfortable. But thanks, honey." She privately resolved to begin her campaign for marriage to Pete immediately. It just might take until the war was over, but she had every confidence that her parents could be won over.

"Whatever you say, babe." Pete put out his cigarette and reached for her again. "I just hope that I can work my way through college and get that doctor's degree. We'll have a good life, doll."

Rita smiled and snuggled up to him. "I'll help you, Pete. And I have a real strong feeling you'll make it, honey. A real strong feeling."

CHAPTER 23

Michael was both shocked and amused. His mother, who was adamantly opposed to Ruth because, among other faults, such as her religion and her lack of social standing, she was considered "fast," was all for Rita Sabrella as her prospective daughter-in-law. He sat in a chair in his home, on a twelve-hour pass from the rehabilitation therapy section of the Oak Knoll Hospital at Oakland, across the bay from San Francisco, and gingerly adjusted his walking cast, bending over and leaning on his crutches for emphasis.

"Mother, I do like Rita—she's a nice girl," he practically shouted at his mother, banging his crutches on the Persian rug as punctuation. "But I love Ruth. And I'm going to marry her and that's it!"

Mary Stratton had been happy enough when she was contacted to drive over to Oakland and bring Michael home for the day, but she became actually excited when she found out on the drive home that Michael had actually met Rita and apparently knew her rather well. Her well-ordered world shook to its very foundations when he said in his next breath, however, that he intended to marry that Braunstein woman. She couldn't believe that her own son could be so utterly shortsighted.

Out of the corner of her eye, she caught sight of a shadow by the door and knew immediately who it was. "Bridget, come in here, please." How humiliating for the help to hear her deluded son speak to her in that manner.

Bridget ran in happily, straight to Michael, who opened his arms wide to her. Mary Stratton suffered a pang of real jealously as she saw the obvious love between the two and spoke even more sharply than she intended.

"May I ask why you were eavesdropping, Bridget?" The tone was glacial.

"Oh, mum. I don't care what it was you were sayin'. I just wanted to greet my boyo here. Our boyo, I mean," she added hastily, glancing at her employer's face. "It's been a long time, mum. For both of us. I am very attached to Michael, Mrs. Stratton. I diapered him when he was a wee babe and I'm certainly entitled to greet him." Her fearless defiance had a good basis. She was indispensable to Mary Stratton in the management of the house, and she knew it. And Mary Stratton knew she knew it. Good help was very difficult to come by these days. Most of the girls went into the shipyards—Rosie the riveter could make much more money than Rosie the housekeeper.

"Oh, very well," and Mary turned aside as the two continued to gush over each other. She knew when she was beaten, though she certainly didn't have to watch them. She wasn't beaten het, however, as far as Michael's choice of a bride was concerned.

Her patience wore thin after another few minutes of waiting. "Well, may I please speak to my own son privately for awhile, Bridget? I would certainly appreciate it."

Bridget looked up at the intended sarcasm, but nothing could mar Michael's homecoming for her. "Certainly, mum. I'm going to tell Cook to put on Michael's favorite, hamburgers with chili."

Just as Mary Stratton was mentally deploring Michael's plebian taste in cuisine, Michael was speaking to Bridget. "No thanks, dear. I'm eating with Ruth tonight. But thanks. It's good to see you, old girl."

"And you're the answer to my prayers, my boy," and Bridget couldn't speak any more. Dabbing at her eyes with her apron, she hurriedly left the room.

"What do you mean, you're eating with Ruth?" his mother demanded. "You haven't even phoned her yet. Do you meant to say I picked you up at the hospital just for the few minutes you've been at home? And you certainly can't drive."

"I phoned her from the hospital, Mother. The Braunsteins invited me over to dinner. I'll just call for a cab to get there and then take a cab back to Oak Knoll to save you the trouble.

Mary Stratton sputtered in frustration a few more minutes, but Michael was already on the telephone, which was conveniently right on the mahogany leather-topped end table placed next to his chair.

"I'm positive the Braunsteins would love to have you for dinner—as part of their family," she said bitterly. She couldn't bring herself to say "their son-in-law." They would probably stop at nothing to . . ."

He interrupted her. "Mother, stop it. As a matter of fact, the Braunsteins were very upset about Ruth's marrying outside of her religion, but they've come around." He saw the disbelief on her face. "That's right, Mother. They've come around to accepting me because they love her and don't want to lose her." He did love his mother, and he knew she loved him. She just wasn't demonstrative, and he knew it was very difficult for her to show that love, which had never been mentioned between them in so many words. "I have to tell you the truth, Mother. I am going to marry Ruth Braunstein, and if it comes to choosing between the two of you . . ." He hated to put it so bluntly, but he was tiring of the same old argument. His leg was bothering him, too. He didn't seem to have the patience he used to have.

Mary Stratton girded up her big guns against her only son. "Have you ever stopped to think about how you will support yourself if you continue on this foolish course? For, of course, you couldn't expect anything from me." Her voice became very low. "Now, or at any time." And then it picked up volume again. "And how will you support a wife? Of course, she's not used to much, but—"

"Don't you worry about that!" he flashed back. "I don't need your money. I'll go to college after the war. Lots of people work their way through. I know Dad made his money in real estate, but Uncle Bill's brokerage firm has always interested me. I could be a broker. I wouldn't mind waiting tables or anything like that." Unfortunately, he couldn't think of any other way to earn money at the moment, although he was reminded of Pete's ambition to become a doctor. It was true that Michael had never had to work a day in his life.

"Besides," he further informed her. "Pete Roffola—you remember Pete—is going with Rita Sabrella, and it seems to be serious. So, you see, even if it weren't for Ruth, Rita and I couldn't have gotten together."

Mary Stratton actually went white. "Pete Ruffola? Isn't he the boy from—from—" She couldn't finish.

"Yes, he's from Butchertown." Michael was even enjoying himself now, experiencing a heady feeling of freedom, though underlying it was sadness about this inevitable estrangement from his mother.

"Excuse me, Mother. I have to go or I'll be late." He pulled himself up and balanced himself on his crutches. Before he left, he turned back hesitantly toward his mother. "I'll see you later, Mother?" It was more a question than a statement.

She nodded curtly. "Of course, Michael. You are my son. I know where my duty lies." Although Mary Stratton would certainly stand by her threat to disinherit her son if he actually married that creature, she hadn't given up her attempt to dissuade him from a step she was convinced would be his ruination. She knew she was an excellent mother, as she had been an excellent wife, and it was her duty to make certain that her son made the right choice.

She watched as Michael quickly and easily swung himself out of the library. He carefully closed the door behind him, first heading from the servants' quarters before he went to his bedroom to clean up. Not only did he want to see Bridget again, but he also wanted to say hello to Annie and Joe. The cook and her husband, who doubled as gardener and sometime chauffeur, had only been with the family for a few years, but he was as fond of them as they were of him. Joe had always wanted to be more of a chauffeur, since he did enjoy driving Mrs. Stratton's Cadillac, but Michael's mother even enjoyed driving Michael's Chrysler convertible, which had been his high school graduation gift. She kept keys to both cars in her possession, using either as convenience and that particular car's supply of gasoline dictated, though Michael only had keys to the Chrysler, of course. If only he had the ability to use the car now, he thought wryly. He realized though that his mother had the ration coupons and that the car's gas supply might be low. Even if he had been able to drive, his pride prevented him from asking her for anything, even gas ration coupons for his own car, under the present circumstances. He wouldn't even ask her if Joe could drive him, although he knew Joe would be happy to do it.

The three of them, Bridget, Annie and Joe, had been waiting for him and converged on him in a boisterous welcome that lifted his spirits considerably as he pumped Joe's hands and kissed the ladies. Realizing, however, that the Yellow Cab that had been called would arrive momentarily, he cut their reunion shorter than he would have liked, and hurried to his room. At last he was going to see Ruth.

CHAPTER 24

If there was a sense of strain at the Braunstein's dinner table in their tiny dining room, Michael and Ruth didn't know it. Their eyes seldom left each other's face, their smiles bathed the whole room with their obvious happiness, and their hands sought each other under the cover of the tablecloth. Etta Braunstein, attired in her good black dress for the occasion, although her slippers somewhat spoiled the effect, sighed as she looked at them. How could anyone resist such joy? Did they think that she and Max couldn't tell they were holding hands under the table when each awkwardly ate with only one hand? She smiled slightly. It was so silly. As if holding hands was a crime! Well, she and Max were resigned to the inevitable if it meant the happiness of their only daughter. But what if it didn't?

Max had been the hard one to win over, and he still wasn't convinced, although he didn't refuse outright. She glanced at him affectionately, thinking how handsome he still was, as he sat at the head of the table in an open-necked yellow sport shirt and brown slacks. He had adamantly refused to wear a tie. That refusal they could all live with. She didn't notice his bald head or his expanding waistline. To Etta he was the slim, handsome young man of thirty-one years ago that she had always thought of as a "Greek god," just as he always saw here as the "zaftig" and curvaceous young brown-haired beauty he had first met in the old country. She had always admired her own mother's vivid red hair and had been ecstatic when Ruth, who had been born balder than her father was now, developed a few strands of the same beautiful hair. She looked with pride at her lovely daughter. She didn't know where those expressive eyes came from— perhaps her great-great grandmother or some other distant ancestor.

When Ruth had first seen Michael push himself out of the Yellow Cab and balance himself precariously on his crutches while he dug down for the taxi fare, her heart seemed to stop. He looked immaculate in his Navy blues and spotless white hat perched jauntily on his black hair. She had been peeking through the window for a good twenty minutes waiting for the first sign of her handsome young sailor. She had showered and dressed herself in a soft green tight-fitting cotton dress that matched her eyes and showed her spectacular figure to its best advantage. She had to use brown leg make-up again with her brown alligator shoes, though. She had already gone through the flat three times, making sure everything looked as nice as possible. For the last ten minutes, while looking through the window, she had convinced herself that she had forgotten what he looked like, but she was afraid to leave the window to check on the photograph he had sent her, for fear she would miss his arrival.

But she had no trouble recognizing him. The doorbell rang and with tact she didn't know her parents possessed, both Max and Etta stayed out of sight while she opened the door. "Hi," she said shyly, berating herself for being unable to think of anything more original. But he just replied in like fashion. "Hi," and they both stood there, smiling at each other.

At last she broke the spell, opening the door wider so that he could enter. "Oh, please come in, Michael. What must you think of me, keeping you outside like that. Oh, and your poor leg!" She forgot her shyness in her concern for his injury, thankful that they lived in the lower flat with only three wide steps to climb up.

As he swung himself over the threshold, he accidentally brushed her in passing, and the electricity was immediate. She was in his arms and the crutches were on the floor while they murmured incoherently to each other.

The wind pushed the door back slightly, pushing Ruth even closer to Michael, and his precarious balance was endangered. She realized his danger immediately and stiffened herself, supporting him while holding him close to her. "Stand still, sweetheart. Being a temporary crutch isn't what I do best. Here, let me get them for you." As he regained his balance and she retrieved the crutches, handing them to him and closing the door, she blushed. She had called him "sweetheart"! She hadn't meant to do that just yet.

"Gee, that sounded good, Ruth. I love to hear you call me 'sweetheart,'—uh, sweetheart," he said softly.

They looked at each other and laughed, both going into a perfect duet of "Let Me Call You Sweetheart," but the laughter changed to kisses in mid-chuckle.

"Let's get to the sofa, honey. Standing on one leg isn't what I do best either, even with a beautiful crutch like you. If we get to the sofa, then maybe we can do what I would like to do best with my best girl," and he added, as he swung himself to the soft, with her right beside him, "or at least one of the things I would like to do best."

She blushed, but murmured, "I think this might be what I do best, too, Michael." But she wouldn't look him in the eyes, instead burying her head on his chest.

They embraced and kissed on a more solid foundation until what started with the utmost tenderness abruptly turned into scarcely-contained passion for both of them. They only had ten minutes, however, until Etta, back in the kitchen with Max, decided that they had enough time already. "Dinner's ready, children," she called. Hearing absolutely no reply, she continued to call every few seconds until she finally heard from her daughter, albeit in a rather shaky voice. "Okay, Mama. We'll be right in," and shortly thereafter they appeared in the kitchen.

No plans had been made by the young couple since talking at the same time as necking was extremely difficult. Other than the obligatory sighs and sounds of love, they had reaffirmed their love and their commitment and, when they were seated in the dining room, they kept holding hands as if by their touch they could prevent any separation ever again.

Etta first served chicken soup with matzo balls, and Michael found to his surprise that he liked it. "This is real good, Mrs. Braunstein," he managed between mouthfuls. Etta beamed, but not too much. This was her daughter involved, and she wasn't going to sell her for a bowl of chicken soup. For his part, Max sat silently and somewhat grimly eating.

Etta couldn't keep quiet for long. "So, Ruth says you were somewhere in a place called New Caledonia?" she asked Michael.

"Yes, Mrs. Braunstein," he responded eagerly. "It's really a beautiful island, but I didn't get to see too much of it. I was in the hospital, of course."

"And how was your trip back with your leg?" Mrs. Braunstein wanted to know.

"It was a hospital ship. Very comfortable and safe. They paint a big red cross on it so the enemy won't attack."

"Hmmph!" Max Braunstein spoke for the first time since he had greeted Michael when he and Ruth entered the kitchen. "I remember World War I. It depends on the enemy."

"Daddy!" Ruth was shocked. "You don't mean that anyone would deliberately attack a hospital ship with wounded men," and her hand unconsciously tightened on Michael's.

"Your father's right, Ruth," Michael said slowly. "Mistakes happen in wartime—and sometimes they're not mistakes."

Max Braunstein gave his prospective son-in-law a grudging glance of approval. At least the boy had some sense.

Etta changed the subject by bringing a steaming pot roast surrounded by onions, potatoes and carrots. "Enjoy, enjoy."

The table conversation gradually reached its normal noisy volume and Etta approvingly noted that Michael enjoyed the give-and-take as much as they did. Eventually, the wedding was discussed at length, although no one could agree on either the time or the place. What finally was agreed was that Sally would be the Maid of Honor and Pete would be Best Man, if hopefully, both were available. Some of the bridesmaids could be Michael's cousins in New York, and some could be Ruth's friends in San Francisco. Ruth definitely wanted her sister-in-law Debbie as a bridesmaid, along with Mrs. Kaminsky. Mrs. Braunstein, however, discouraged the idea of Mrs. Kaminsky vehemently, saying she was too old. Ruth realized, as after a few protestations that age was no barrier to being a bridesmaid or a friend, that her mother was actually jealous of her friendship with the older woman, and diplomatically dropped the subject for the moment.

Max brought up one of the big questions he and Etta had been concerned about and blurted out, gruffly but not unpleasantly, "And who is to perform this wedding?"

Silence reigned again. Michael offered weakly, "Could we have both a rabbi and a minister? Would that be possible?"

Etta replied shortly, "Rabbis don't marry mixed couples. I don't know about ministers."

Ruth was thinking hard. She had been thinking about the answer to that question almost since she had received Michael's proposal, and she had investigated several possibilities. "I have this girlfriend, Rose Shapiro," she began slowly. "And she's going with an Irish soldier. He hasn't proposed to her yet, but she found out that a Unitarian minister would marry them if he did propose."

Etta was thoughtful. "So Rose Shapiro is so anxious even before the boy proposes. Don't worry, Ruth, why should I tell her mother? I won't, I won't," as her daughter gave her a look she knew well. "Unitarian? Yes, I think I've heard of that, too." She turned pleadingly to Max. "Max? It would be under God, Max. And it would be legal, wouldn't it? Wouldn't that be better than a Justice of the Peace in Reno? As long as they're getting married . . ."

Max was defeated, and he knew it. He was defeated by the love in his own family and by the love that was so obvious between the young couple. "Okay, okay, whatever you want is all right by me." He spoke even more gruffly than usual, and only Etta noticed that there was a bit of moisture in his eyes. "You just make her happy, young fellow. You hear me?"

Michael was immensely relieved. "Yes, sir, I certainly will," and it was the easiest promise he had ever made. He had every confidence in their future happiness.

Once again many voices at once cheerfully rang out around the table, and a party atmosphere subtly made itself known, which was even more evident when Mrs. Braunstein brought homemade chocolate cake to the table. It, too, tasted delicious to Michael—but then the entire evening was delicious to him.

Michael and Ruth offered to do the dishes, and Mrs. Braunstein graciously accepted, leaving the kitchen to the two young people. Michael had never dried dishes before, but, as Ruth showed him, the operation was a simple one, and he enjoyed "playing house" with Ruth. Just as they were finishing up a highly successful washing-and-drying operation, Michael asked Ruth when he could see her again.

"I have to go to bed early tomorrow night, since tonight won't be too early. Will it?" and she looked at him flirtatiously.

"No way, honey."

"So, then, the day after tomorrow?"

"That's great, sweetheart." Michael knew he could get a pass easily enough, but then realized he had no access to his car. Taking cabs once in awhile was fine, but it could eat up his rather meager salary very quickly if it were done on a permanent basis, especially to and from Oakland. And then suddenly he got an idea. Whether it was practical or not, however, depended entirely on her answer to his next question.

"Ruth, can you drive?" He knew the family had no car, but he was hoping.

"Yes, I can," she answered proudly. "My brother David taught me. He and Debbie have this 1932 Ford, and he gave me lessons, although I haven't driven for awhile now."

"Do you have a driver's license?" Everything was going so sell, he held his breath.

"Yes." She turned, puzzled, to look at him. "What's all this about, Michael?"

He gave a war-whoop and grabbed her to him, the one crutch he had under his arm while he was drying the dishes clattering to the floor. "Honey, you're going to get a lot more practice!"

"Michael! My parents will be running in here with all this racket!" But she was laughing at his exuberance and embracing him in return.

"Honey, you remember my car?"

"Sure. But you can't drive! Oh, you want me to drive it!"

"That's my smart girl! You can drive me back and forth. But wait a minute, I didn't think." He hesitated. "Is this an imposition, honey? Maybe it would be too much for you. Oh, I'm asking too much."

"No, no, Michael. I'd be happy to do it. That would solve our problem, wouldn't it?" She then hesitated. "But I haven't driven for a year—and to tell you the truth, I'm not very good at it. Do you think I could drive it?"

"Oh, sweetie, you'll be great. I'll give you a refresher course, and you'll be just fine. We could take a cab to the house the day after tomorrow to get the car together, right after you get off work, and I'll be right alongside you." We could go other places too that way, wherever we want. Are you sure, Ruthie? You really don't mind?"

"Oh Michael, I'm so glad to do it for you. Anyway, I would be doing it for us, wouldn't I?" She embraced him lovingly. "But what about the gas? Do you have ration coupons for the car?"

He calmed down somewhat. "Don't worry about the ration coupons, honey. I'll get them."

He had decided that pride was fine, but not when it interfered with the practical matters of real life, and that he would ask his mother for the coupons. No one had mentioned his mother during dinner, and he guessed that the Braunsteins had been briefed by Ruth as to the problems there. Something had to be done about that. His mother had to receive Ruth and she had to meet the Braunsteins. That was the next step.

CHAPTER 25

"No, No, No!!!" Michael was shouting at the top of his lungs. This was much more terrifying than the sinking of the Lady Lex.

"You don't have to yell at me, Michael," retorted Ruth, with tears in her eyes and voice as she swerved sharply. "You could just say 'no' calmly, you know."

Michael looked at the one car parked on the quiet street that Ruth had missed by the smallest fraction and sat back again, temporarily relieved. "I'm sorry, honey." He seemed to be saying that a lot lately—but he had never realized how difficult it was to teach someone no matter how dear, to drive, someone who obviously had no talent for it, regardless of where else her talents did lie. Already Ruth had threatened to get out of the car—in the middle of the highway—and walk home. It was then he had suggested this quiet street. "I'm sorry," he repeated, "but there was only one car on the whole block. You did say you'd had some lessons from your brother?"

"I told you it's been a long time. I know I'm not a good driver, but I'm doing the best I can with the equipment I have!" She grimly turned the wheel so that they were on the correct side of the street again.

"Honey, your equipment is the best—but not for driving." He couldn't see how she had passed her driving test. "Uhh—when did you take your road test?" He used all the diplomacy at his command.

She looked at him sharply. He screamed and he looked back just in time to avoid going up onto the sidewalk. "I know what you mean, Michael," she said.

"I hate driving. I took the damn test three times before I passed. I think the instructor was sorry for me." Then she smiled. "I passed the written test 100% though!"

She cast a quick look at his appalled face and began to laugh. He had to join her, and she quickly pulled the car as near to the curb as she could manage and did all the proper things to stop the car. They leaned against each other as they both giggled helplessly.

When Michael had braved his mother to ask for the gas ration coupons, he had no idea that that was the easy part. He had told her a friend was going to keep the car for him and drive him around, and to his surprise, she handed the coupons over without a murmur. Thankfully, she didn't ask who the friend was, and he had no way of knowing that she had decided to give in to him on the smaller issues so that she would have more leverage with the very large one of who he was going to marry. She did mention, so that he would be aware of her sacrifice, that sometimes she liked to drive the convertible herself, especially downtown, where it was harder to find a parking space for the large Cadillac. The extra ration coupons certainly came in handy, especially on Saturday nights like tonight, when she was going to the USO to do her part for the war effort. So she handed them over to him without argument. He was appreciative, more than she knew. And it was a perfect night for her to be out of the house, since he had to bring Ruth there in a cab to pick up the car.

As Ruth and Michael gradually stopped laughing, they began kissing, and they hugged each other as tightly as possible in the cramped front seat, but the gears made it very difficult. They looked at each other, still smiling. "You know, Michael," Ruth said shyly, "If we can get through these refresher courses without breaking up, we can get through anything."

"I'm inclined to agree with you, darling." Michael wouldn't risk any further conversation that wasn't essential to the driving process. "Oh, by the way, before we start again, I wanted to tell you that I phoned my uncle in New York and told him about us."

"Oh that's great, Michael. What did he say?" Ruth was understandably wary, given her experience with Mrs. Stratton.

"He congratulated me and wishes you the best," Michael responded proudly. Ruth relaxed. "He really seemed happy for us, Ruthie. He's a great guy. And my Aunt Catherine wished us the best, too. They're both tops."

"Oh, I am glad." And that was the understatement of the year, Ruth thought.

"I also told him I was interested in the brokerage business," Michael went on casually. "And Uncle Bill offered to set me up in San Francisco after I finish college."

"Michael! Why didn't you tell me before? This is absolutely marvelous! I can keep my job while you're attending college, and—"

Michael smiled at her enthusiasm. "Love of my life, I've been very involved with your driving—or haven't you noticed? Anyway, I was saving it for a surprise." This was a good time, he thought, to make up for all that screaming at her. "What's more," and his hand tightened on hers to give her the rest of the good news, "he said he always wanted a branch in San

Francisco, but he needed someone he could trust—and that's me, of course!"

Ruth was overwhelmed. "So, you'll be a stock-broker. Don't you need to go to school for that, too, besides college?"

"Oh, college isn't essential for stockbrokers, but I agree with Uncle Bill and my mother that I do need more education. Then he says I can learn the business with some of his friends here and when I'm ready—kazam! I take the broker's test and there I am!"

The two smiled at each other, their bliss complete, their future assured. As Michael steeled himself for another "refresher course," he thought only of Ruth and their future together, with only the faint cloud of his disapproving mother to mar his happiness.

CHAPTER 26

Michael was desperate. It had been two months, and his mother was still adamant in her objection to Ruth. He had slowly come to realize that she would never give her approval to his marrying the girl he loved.

His mother had even suggested, ever so delicately, that he "wouldn't have to marry that woman in order to—," and she cleared her throat meaningfully. He became furious and stormed out of the house, but he returned that evening. He really didn't want a break with his mother. He would do all he could to avoid that. He had learned one thing when he was in combat along with the other swabbies. Each man rose to the best or worst in himself. She couldn't help being as she was any more than he could help being what he was.

What his mother couldn't understand was that he really loved Ruth. Ruth had even offered herself to him one evening when they were parked at the furthest point of Ocean Beach, as far away from the other parked cars as they could get. Her eyes were shining with selfless love, and he knew that she was not only motivated by passion, but also by her desire to give him her ultimate gift. With his entire body crying for release, he surprised himself by refusing. He also knew that she really wanted marriage, and he loved her enough to give her the gift of waiting.

Everything else was working out well. His leg had healed to the extent that he had completely dispensed with the cast and the crutches. He did have a definite limp, but it wasn't too bad, considering. Now that he was released from the hospital, he was starting his thirty-day sunken ship leave. It was a perfect time to get married.

Desperate situations called for desperate measure. Why not get married? He could drive now, thank God, and they could make it up to Reno in about five hours. He certainly wouldn't trust Ruth to drive that distance. They hadn't actually used many gasoline ration coupons at all so far, because, although they enjoyed each other thoroughly, neither of them enjoyed her driving.

When Michael made up his mind, he acted upon it. They would get married as quickly as possible so they could take full advantage of his month-long leave. Once they were married, his mother would have to accept her. There would be nothing else she could do.

He found an unexpected obstacle, however, in Ruth herself. Ruth remembered all too well what her mother had said when she was pleading with her father to accept the idea of a Unitarian minister marrying them. She knew her parents' hearts would be broken if she ran away to Reno and if she didn't have a conventional wedding with her father giving her away and her mother crying. And, to tell the truth, she rather wanted that sort of wedding, too. She didn't want a quickie ceremony with strangers that didn't know or care for them. She didn't know if she would feel married that way.

At last they reached a compromise, although Michael didn't quite know how it was going to work out. They wouldn't tell Ruth's parents that they were going to be married in Reno. They would only tell Michael's mother when they returned so that she would have to accept the inevitable. Then, later, they would have a big wedding with everyone and his brother so Mr. and Mrs. Braunstein would be happy. The only glitch was in Mrs. Stratton's keeping the Reno marriage secret from the Braunsteins. Since she had absolutely no contact with them and obviously didn't wish any, it might work out.

"But I have a thirty-day leave, Ruthie," Michael protested. "We could have a real honeymoon!"

"What happens after that, darling?" Ruthie couldn't bear to think of him leaving again. "With that leg, they surely won't send you into battle again. Will they?"

"Oh, I'll probably have a safe assignment somewhere. After all, I can't run that fast any more, you know!" He tried to make a joke out of it, but neither laughed this time. "I'll find out when my leave is over, Ruthie."

Ruth was thinking quickly. "Okay, honey. I'll ask my folks to set up a wedding date in—say, a week. They'll scream, but I guess they can phone enough people to set up a real wedding. There's a war on, after all. I'm due one week's vacation at work, but when I tell them I'm marrying an American hero, I'm sure I can get a few more weeks off. Then we'll have three weeks."

"Oh, we could have more than that, my love. We do have the car, you know," and Michael leered at her.

They were sitting in the convertible at the time. Ruth blushed, giggled, and shifted so that the gearshift wasn't sticking into her leg. "This itty bitty space? How?" It was difficult enough necking there, although there were times when they were completely oblivious to the cramped quarters.

"Leave everything to me, sweetheart." Michael was ebullient. "We'll manage. In fact, I'll arrange it all."

And he did, even down to a wedding dinner at the Fairmont Hotel, a hotel considered to be the finest in San Francisco, although he did like the Top of the Mark at the Mark Hopkins across the street, where you could get a great view of the city. Well, they could get a drink there first.

* * *

Ruth was so excited she could hardly stand it as she dressed by the light of her bedside lamp early Sunday morning. She did feel guilty about deceiving her parents, telling them that she and Michael were going to the Sacramento State Fair and would be away all day, but she told herself that they would never know where they were really heading, so they wouldn't be hurt. The only people she had told about her plans were Sally and Mrs. Kaminsky. Mrs. Kaminsky already knew before she opened her mouth and Sally wanted to go with them and stand up for them. Michael had said, however, that it would be better for them to be by themselves (and Ruth had a good idea of what he meant), but she would certainly be Ruth's Maid of Honor at their official wedding. Michael would be calling for her soon, at 6:00 a.m.

She chose her wedding outfit carefully. She didn't have a white, dressy dress, so she made do with her best, a beige rayon dress so beautifully made it looked like silk, a dress that showed off her large, well-shaped breasts and emphasized her tiny waist, and her beige sandals that added two inches to her height. Sally, a true friend, had generously given Ruth her only pair of nylon stockings, and Ruth put them on carefully. September was just a little cool in San Francisco in the evening, although it was hot in Reno, so she added a beige light wool coat and brown leather gloves, and she placed a tiny matching veiled pillbox hat jauntily down on her shining red hair. She knew she looked her best. A white wedding dress was what she would wear in her second wedding, and she giggled as she thought how she was reversing the "virgin in white" tradition. At any rate, her panties, bra, and slip were white, all brand new and the laciest and prettiest that The White House had to offer. She blushed as the thought went through her mind that the white of her lingerie was nearer to what was presently virgin territory, anyway.

She waved her left hand gracefully in the air as she looked into the mirror, admiring the flash made by the small diamond in the white gold band. Michael had wanted to buy her a much bigger engagement ring, but she liked the delicate workmanship on this one, and besides, he would have to pay it off at Samuel's Jewelers with his Navy salary if he wasn't to send up any alarms to his mother. Ruth wanted to help, but he wouldn't hear of it. Ruth had been so impressed when they had walked over from The Emporium on Market Street, where they had been window shopping, to the elegant jewelry store with the huge clock in front, and even more impressed when he casually said, "Charge it, please," after they'd selected it.

Her choice of clothing was definitely not what she would have chosen to visit the Sacramento State Fair, but her mother was still asleep and hopefully would remain that way as she tiptoed out. Although her mother would immediately notice the discrepancy between the way she was dressed and her supposed destination, her adoring father would just think she "looked nice." With any luck, they would both be asleep when she returned home in the wee hours tomorrow. Even if her mother came into her room to make certain she was safe, as was her wont, she would be safely asleep in her nightgown and not in her telltale "wedding dress."

Michael pulled up just as she was quietly closing the front door, and they both took it as a good omen that neither had to wait. Michael, dressed in a new navy blue tailor-made uniform, with his campaign ribbons proudly displayed, and his spotless white hat set at a rakish angle, was as excited as Ruth, and his blue eyes were just as delighted as her green eyes when they smiled at each other.

They spoke in unison. "Michael, you look so great!" "Ruthie, you're so damn beautiful!" And they laughed again as Michael got out of the car to help Ruth in on her side with a flourish, a kiss and a hug.

"We're a handsome couple, sweetie. You know that!" Michael beamed. He slowly began closing Ruth's door, being a trifle too solicitous in making sure her coat didn't get caught in the door as he tucked it around, under and over her.

She caught his wandering hand and kissed it. "Well, I'm sure glad this handsome couple is so handy, my Michael. I wouldn't have it any other way." But still she held his hand, looking quickly up and down the street and then smiling provocatively at Michael. He laughed, turned over her hand, and kissed hers, finally closing her door. Smiling, she watched him go back to his side. He was such a gentleman, and he was such a rogue, and she loved him so.

Only one thing bothered her now, and typically, she plunged right into the problem. Ruth wasn't much one for small talk. "Michael," she began hesitantly. "This day sounds so wonderful. It's like a dream come true. I do love you so. But to see your mother and confront her afterwards—that would be like a nightmare for me after the dream. I've told you how she made it clear at the USO that she didn't like me, no matter what I did. I just don't know how to make her like me," and she stopped, unable to go on for a moment. "And I can't help it spoiling the dream a bit. Could we—could we see her later—not today? Please?" She waited breathlessly for his answer.

A shadow passed over Michael's handsome face. He hadn't thought of that. Of course it would be painful for Ruth tonight. Tonight was her wedding night, their wedding night, by God, the whole day and night were going to be great. "Sweetheart, you're absolutely right. Today's our day, and only our day. I'm sorry, Ruthie. I just didn't think. We'll see Mother later."

"Oh Michael, my Michael, thank you!" Ruth said, now completely relieved. It took more than five hours from the time Michael actually started the car and began the long drive that was to change their lives, but the time passed quickly. They always seemed to have something to say to each other, remarking on the spectacular scenery or planning their future, but even when they were quietly sitting side by side, they were happy with each other.

* * *

The newlyweds, Mr. and Mrs. Michael Stratton, were dining at the Fairmont Hotel in San Francisco. They had started their celebration with a Planter's Punch for Ruth and a scotch and soda for Michael at the Top of the Mark across the street. It was the first time Ruth had ever been in a bar, but although she was only nineteen, she knew she looked at least twenty-two, and it seemed to her that a married woman should be able to drink if she wished. Michael recommended the Planter's Punch, which was loaded with fruit juice, and she like it, though the rum burned her throat a bit. She discovered she wasn't much of a drinker when she began feeling dizzy when she had finished about a third of the drink, and left the rest. Her green eyes grew wide as she admired the amazing view of her city, which grew more spectacular with every sip. All around her were servicemen and their ladies, with a few servicewomen here and there. The only civilians, that night at any rate, were the elderly, dignified waiters.

When they made their way across the street to the Fairmont, even more imposing than the Mark Hopkins, Ruth thought the luxurious furnishings, the magnificent chandeliers, the spacious rooms could have come right out of a castle in a fairytale.

The wedding itself had been simple and wonderful. To Ruth's surprise, the ceremony wasn't performed by a Justice of the Peace. Michael had arranged for a Unitarian minister at a tiny chapel. He was a wonderful old man, and his darling little wife and her two adorable sisters stood up for them. The whole world was friendly and marvelous for the two lovers. Michael had produced a wedding ring that matched the engagement ring perfectly, which would reside on

Ruth's third finger of her left hand until they had to part and go to their respective homes. He had even thought of that, however. He also produced, after the ceremony when they were alone, a white gold chain to hang the ring around her neck until they could be married again.

They wandered around Reno for about an hour, just looking and holding hands, awed by the wonder of their new lives. They stopped in a little coffee shop, but neither could eat much. And the five hours back were even more wonderful than the trip to their future had been.

Michael was ordering for them now, a veritable banquet. It was pretty expensive, but after all, this was their wedding feast. At least the first one. Michael had chosen the New York steak, which ran $2.50 for the complete dinner, while Ruth had baked lobster in the half shell thermador, which was $1.75. The entire dinner consisted of an appetizer, which for Ruth was crab flakes with avocado and for Michael, Olympic oyster cocktail, and celery and olives, mock turtle soup, corn sauté, Parisienne potatoes, new peas buerre, and gourmet salad for both of them. For dessert, they were served Peach Melba with strawberry sauce for Ruth and coffee ice cream and cake for Michael, with demi tasse and mints for both after dinner. Ruth was glad she hadn't eaten much else during the day. They were serenaded throughout their superb dinner by Ernie Heckscher's lilting music and got up for one wedding dance.

"Everything is just so perfect," Ruth whispered in Michael's ear as he whirled her around the dance floor.

"My love, I will now show you how you can be happier," Michael replied, dissolving Ruth into helpless giggles. He led her off the floor and paid their bill, then they took the elevator up to their room. "I'd scoop you up over the threshold in a heartbeat," he said, looking down at his leg, "but . . ."

"It's quite all right, my husband," Ruth said tenderly. He bowed to her and took her hand, leading her into the room. Michael had thought of everything. There was a bouquet of yellow roses and a bucket with champagne waiting in the candlelit room.

"Husband. I like hearing you say that, Ruth, my wife," Michael replied.

Ruth discovered that making love was even more wonderful than she had imagined, and Michael discovered that, although lust was certainly part of love, there was a world of difference between the two. His tender passion for Ruth took him to new heights.

After their love had consumed them and they lay at rest, quietly savoring each other, they each had the same fearful thought. They both remembered too well what the doctor had told Ruth's mother so long ago, that she could never have a "normal' life. There had been absolutely no indication of any tragic disruption of their love, no indication of any fatigue on Ruth's part. Their eyes met, and they knew each other's thought.

It's okay, Michael," Ruth said softly when she realized all was well. "The doctor really didn't know what he was talking about. Thank God, it's okay." She knew, she just knew, it would all be fine. Then she smiled. "Actually, sweetheart, it was quite a bit better than okay. It was—it was—" She couldn't think of a word great enough to fit the occasion. "It was pure love," she finally whispered. He couldn't have agreed more.

CHAPTER 27

Pete had found a French Catholic priest who would marry them. Not secretly, for the priest gave him a lecture on the problems that could arise from clandestine weddings, but quietly and discretely. Just so the Navy wouldn't find out. The priest was an understanding one. Now to see how Rita would take this. Pete had fully committed himself, heart and soul, and he saw no use in waiting to make it legal. He knew she loved him, too, but there were depths in Rita he didn't quite understand. Although, he thought smugly, there were also depths he sure was familiar with. He wondered why she was late. He had been waiting at the French inn for ten minutes now. What was keeping her?

At that moment, Rita swept toward their booth, and Pete's heart turned over. She still had that power over him. And to look at her and the light in her eyes, it was reciprocated. He had it all planned how to approach the subject of their wedding. She didn't seem anxious to get married at all.

"I couldn't get here any earlier, honey," she said breathlessly. She sat down and he closed the curtain quickly around the booth. "We had an emergency and all the nurses were needed. I came as quickly as I could. And I can't stay, sweetheart. I've got to go right back. I only came to tell you."

He winced. "What ship got it?"

"I honestly don't know at this point, Pete. All I know is that I have a lot of broken men to take care of," and a shadow passed over her face. "How long is this damn war going to last, anyway?"

He looked at her tenderly. Lines were on her pretty face that hadn't been there two months ago. "I don't know either, Babe. You'd think we were a couple of enemy agents, the way we don't know nothing—I mean, anything." Rita had been tactfully and privately coaching him in English toward the time he would be her parents' son-in-law, fortunately a time far into the future, she thought, since he needed a great deal more tutoring.

Pete cleared his throat. He began his campaign. He pulled a letter from his pocket and mentioned, very casually, "I just got a letter from Mike."

Rita was instantly suspicious. One of the things she loved about him was his transparency. "What's up, darlin'?"

"Take a look at the letter." But before she could read it, he told her. "The kids are getting secretly married, Babe. His old lady doesn't like his girl, so he figured that if they were married, she'd have to accept her."

"That doesn't make a whole lot of sense, Pete," she responded, puzzled. "Why secretly? If they keep it a secret from his mama, his mama won't know about it!"

"They're not keeping it a secret from his mother, sweetie. They're going to tell her. They're keeping it a secret from Ruth's folks, because they're all set up for a big wedding and they don't want to disappoint them."

"Oh. Well, I can see why, then. It's too bad you can't be at the weddin', honey."

"Yeah, I'd really like to go. And Mike wants me, too. But I was thinking about another wedding, Rita."

“Oh?” Pete never called her Rita unless he was deadly serious.

“Our wedding, honey. I was thinking of sort of a double wedding.”

She became alarmed. “What are you talkin’ about, Pete? How can we have any sort of wedding, much less a double wedding? And with what other couple?”

“Mike and Ruth, of course. Haven’t you been listening?” Rita looked at him as she would have looked at one of her patients. “I know we can’t really get married along with them, Babe. But we could get married the same way they did—secretly—and about the same time. That’s sort of a double wedding, ain’t—isn’t it?” And then he told her the topper. “I found a French Catholic priest who will marry us and the Navy will never know nothing about it.” In his excitement he forgot his grammar lessons, but Rita didn’t even notice. Something he had said about Michael’s letter stuck in her mind. She opened it and read it. Carefully.

When she finished, her eyes were bright. “I do think that can be arranged, darlin’,” she said softly. Pete gave out a whoop that could be heard on the other side of the island. Rita laughed. “If you don’t quiet down, darlin’, we won’t be going to the priest. We’ll be going to the looney bin!”

Michael had said in his letter that his mother would have to accept them once he and Ruth were married. Why not get married to Pete? Her parents had proven remarkably recalcitrant. Once she and Pete were married, they would have no choice, just like Michael’s mother. Of course, Pete could never know this. She wanted him and his parents to get along. If he ever found out they objected to him, he would never forget it. As far as he was concerned, there was only the problem with that stupid regulation that forbade enlisted personnel to fraternize with officers—and a marriage between her and Pete definitely fell into that category. Michael's letter to Pete really did give him—and her—a great idea. He just might have solved the entire problem, not only with the Navy, but also with her stubborn parents, whom she loved to distraction. But she loved Pete even more.

At that moment, their favorite waitress came to take their order. Although Rita was preparing to return to the hospital, Pete ordered coffee, feeling very content. At first amazed, he was now complacently congratulating himself on his persuasive abilities.

CHAPTER 28

"Could you please tell me why it is so necessary for you to inflict this woman on me?" Mrs. Stratton asked Michael in a reasonable tone.

"Mother!" Michael was almost at the point of no return. "I have told you time and time again that I love 'this woman,' as you put it. We have something to tell you, something we must tell you together." Surely she would have to accept the situation when they stood before her as man and wife. It was difficult to believe that anyone could look upon Ruthie and be exposed to her genuinely warm, caring personality and not grow fond of her. It was his last desperate move to save his badly deteriorating relationship with his mother, although, of course, they had never really been close. He hated to inflict this upon Ruth, that's what he hated to do.

Mary Stratton was most alarmed. What could they possibly have to tell her together? Perhaps she should make herself available so that she would be able to properly combat whatever threat this posed.

"Very well," she replied slowly. "I will make myself available to you and that woman tonight. I expect you both at 7:00."

"Seven? Can't it be later, Mother? Ruth gets off work at 6:00, and—" Michael was so relieved his mother had finally given in that it gave him hope for a more reasonable hour so that he and Ruth could find some privacy first. It had been awhile.

Mrs. Stratton coldly interrupted him. "Seven, Michael. I don't intend to spoil my entire evening." And then she stalked out of the room.

Michael stood there, aghast. He knew his mother had absolutely nothing else to do that evening. It wouldn't matter what time Ruth came over. Well, nothing to do but phone Ruthie at work and tell her to develop a headache so that she could leave the store early.

As he was making his way toward the phone, Bridget bustled in, looking back warily over her shoulder as she entered.

"Oh, Bridget!" He really needed Bridget at this moment, and he embraced her warmly. Bridget's hand, complete with duster, patted Michael comfortingly on the back.

"There, there, me darlin'," and Bridget dropped the duster completely. "I know what's been goin' on, that I do."

"You know?" He stepped back and looked affectionately at his old comrade. "Now, how do you know? And just what exactly do you know?"

"I know the old lady isn't about to accept your lady love, that's what I know. And I know you're both comin' here tonight to confront her," and then she burst out with, "and I wish I would know how to make things right for you, my boy, that I do!"

"Well, I see listening at the door has paid off, my friend," Michael attempted to speak lightly. "But you just haven't listened enough, or at the right door."

"Whatever do you mean?" Bridget bristled in mock indignation.

"Well, I'll tell you, old girl." Michael lowered his voice. "We're married, Bridget. Ruth and I were married last Sunday in Reno."

He waited for the delight to show in her face, and he wasn't disappointed. Unfortunately, the tears began to fall at the same time.

"Oh, my boy, my boy," she sobbed. "And I wasn't there to see it. But I am so happy for you, Michael. You love the lass and you wanted her, and by all the saints, now you have her. But I wasn't there to see it, my boy!"

Now he tried to comfort her. "Shhh, Bridget, shhhh. Don't cry. Besides, all is not lost. We're going to be married again, you see, and you can come to that one."

Bridget listened spellbound as Michael explained the circumstances that necessitated their plan. "Now remember, not a word of this to Mother or anyone else. Ruth and I will tell Mother in a last-ditch attempt to get her approval, but Ruthie's parents must never know or they would really be hurt. They're good people, Bridget. You'd like them." And she really would, he thought.

"Of course, of course now," Bridget regained control of herself and blew her nose briskly. "Now would you be after anyone who wasn't the best and from the best? My lips are sealed, my boy, don't worry about that. Have I ever betrayed you?" And she gave him a wink that warmed him as he continued toward the phone to call Ruthie.

* * *

Ruth really did have a headache as she tried on yet another dress in her limited wardrobe. She had left work three hours early, and all of her time, after her second shower of the day, had been spent on choosing and discarding most of her clothes and combination of clothes. She wanted something very conservative, something that wouldn't make Mrs. Stratton any angrier than she was, and she didn't think she had anything that conservative in her closet.

Then she remembered a gray suit she had bought when she started to work under the delusion that her working attire should be severe and plain. She only wore the suit once, because she just didn't feel right in it, and she went back to clothes that made her feel more comfortable. She finally found it in Etta's closet. Etta was going to use the material to make something or other. She sighed in relief. Once properly pressed, this would be perfect. It did absolutely nothing for her. She must tell Michael to look at her as seldom as possible, however.

She was so nervous. At least keeping busy helped that. She thought she would like to drive to his house tonight. She would be kept so busy keeping on the road that maybe she wouldn't think about what awaited her there. And why was Michael calling for her at 5:30 sharp when his mother said to be there at 7:00? She blushed, smiling. He probably wanted to park in their favorite spot. She hoped it wouldn't muss up her suit. But she looked forward to their parking as much as he did.

As she was hurriedly ironing her suit, her mother called to her again. She had been asking questions about the wedding constantly.

"So, what kind of flowers do you want to carry?" Etta looked both harassed and happy. Ruth thought fondly that this was what her mother needed to take her mind off their loss. And, with the thought of Jerry, a shadow passed over her own face.

"Mama, I think the groom is supposed to supply the flowers. You don't have to worry about that. You have enough to think about."

"Do I have enough to think about? Do I have enough to think about? Do I have to get a wedding ready in one week? A wedding with people, yet? A wedding with food I haven't cooked yet? A wedding with a Unitarian minister, who, thank God, I've got already?" and Etta Braunstein, still happily complaining, went back to the phone to call yet another friend.

When Ruth finally had the gray suit on, she really didn't look so bad, she thought to herself. She had put on her gray lizard sandals with the two-inch heels. They were sexy, true, but maybe Mrs. Stratton wouldn't notice her feet, and she had to have something to keep up her self-confidence. She had no coat, hat, or gloves that would match, but one didn't need a coat with a suit anyway, and she would just do without a hat or gloves.

She was just finished dressing when the doorbell rang, and she ran to the door just as her mother was asking if she and Michael wanted to invite his New York relatives. "I'll bring you a list of Michael's side, Mama. Don't worry about it."

The last she heard as she went down the stairs with Michael was, "I shouldn't worry about it? I shouldn't—" and the door closed.

CHAPTER 29

As Ruth and Michael pulled up to the Stratton home, Ruth was giggling and Michael chuckling over their escapade. Ruth had the naughty thought that what they did was the best way to keep busy, much better than driving, to forget Mrs. Stratton. The problem didn't even enter their minds.

"Oh, Michael," she murmured. "Right in broad daylight! What if someone had seen us? And getting our clothes on again in that little front seat—it was a wonder I didn't put your eye out when my elbow hit you!"

"No one saw us," he replied smugly. "And even if they did, we're man and wife aren't we? We're also lucky I didn't kick you when I was putting on my pants. At any rate, your suit looks like new."

"It was a good thing I put it over the seat. But—it was wonderful, Michael."

"Yes, sweetheart wife, it was wonderful." It really was, but now they must return to the real world, he thought grimly, as he got out of the car and held the door for her. "Did you take the wedding ring off the chain and put it back on your finger, honey?"

She held it up for him to see. "I wouldn't forget that, darling." She added hesitantly, "Michael, would you please not leave me alone with her? Please?"

"I promise, Ruthie. Now, let's get it over with." They went up to the ornate front door, where Michael let them in with his key. It was just 7:00 p.m.

He stood aside for her to enter first, saying out of nervousness more than anything else, as he looked around, "Gee, the good old San Francisco fog is right on schedule. It's going to be like pea soup later."

Ruth just replied, "Mmmm . . ." Neither one had any real interest in the fog at the moment.

The first person they encountered was Bridget, who without a word, turned to Ruth and embraced her. Ruth was startled at first, then gratefully and enthusiastically returned the hug. "You're Bridget!" she said unnecessarily.

"And who else would I be, now?" Bridget beamed at her. "You just remember old Bridget's on your side, my girl, and maybe that might help you with the old lady a bit." She was right. The memory of that warm welcome did help with the icy reception she was about to endure.

Mary Stratton was seated in the library, waiting for them. Dressed all in gray, with sensible flat oxfords, with her white hair and pale complexion, she seemed colorless. She had not bothered to put on any makeup at all for the occasion, and looked and felt very much the beleaguered and long-suffering mother. She looked at her watch as they came in. It was two minutes after 7:00.

Michael said nothing about the difference in time. He had been defensive long enough. He cleared his throat. "Mother."

"Yes, Michael?" She did not acknowledge Ruth at all.

"You know Ruth, don't you?" Michael went on, determined to force her to acknowledge his wife.

Mrs. Stratton still did not look at Ruth, but she did say "Yes" to Michael.

"Well, Mother," Michael felt as if he and Ruth were naughty children, standing in front of his mother hand-in-hand, and perhaps that pushed him to be more abrupt than usual. "Ruth and I are now married. We are man and wife."

Absolute and complete silence greeted that announcement. His mother couldn't believe it. She finally glanced coldly at Ruth, who was standing as close to Michael as she could, desperately clinging to his hand.

"What did you say?"

"I said, Mother, that Ruth and I are married. We went to Reno on Sunday and got married." He softened his tone, pleading just a little. "We want to be friends with you, Mother. Please accept the woman I love."

The words, "the woman I love," reminded Ruth of the same words that were spoken by King Edward VIII of England, who gave up his throne for the woman he loved, Wally Simpson, a few years ago. Was Michael really giving up too much for her?

His mother looked at him with contempt. "You have always shown poor judgment, Michael. You do seem to be obsessed with lower-class people, such as our servant. You insisted on joining the Navy as an enlisted man, though I could have easily have arranged it so that you could have some status as an officer. And now this!"

Michael felt Ruth trembling beside him. "Mother!" he raged, protesting, but she went on.

There was really nothing more to say. But his mother went on and on and on. Everything that he had done during his youth and childhood that she didn't like, every friend she disapproved of, every statement he had made and had now forgotten, were all dredged up. She wouldn't be interrupted, though

Michael tried. Ruth was only still there because of Michael and Michael's hand, which he clasped protectively over her smaller one. And Michael was only there because of a forlorn hope against all odds that, when she finally finished her litany of complaints, that she would relent.

After fifteen minutes of a tirade that had been delivered in a reasonable tone of voice, which somehow proved to be more hurtful, she stood up.

"Do you know what you have driven your mother to, Michael?" she accused him. "Your own mother, who raised you alone, fatherless, and gave you the best that money could buy. I was advised, after your father died, to place you in a foster home so that I could better pursue my own interests, but no, I did not. I kept you and raised you."

This self-aggrandizing pronouncement shocked Ruth more than anything else on that terrible evening. To even imagine giving up your own child was beyond her comprehension. And to congratulate herself for not giving him up!

"You have driven me from my own house tonight," Michael's mother continued. "I will not stay in this house with that woman another minute. I am going to the Club for a few hours to meet with cultured people, people of our own class. By the way, Michael," and she turned to administer the coup de grace. "I suppose you realize that, if you do not divorce, you will never be able to bring your wife there. They do not allow Jews, you know. You must consider what it will be like to have a Jewish wife if you persist in this foolishness. Your career, your very life, will be restricted."

Ruth's face grew white as Michael's flushed. They seemed to be frozen in time, standing there, unable to move.

Mary Stratton picked up her purse from the end table beside her. She turned once more to Michael before she left. "If you are wise, by the time I return tonight, you will have decided to get a divorce. I don't suppose an annulment is possible, knowing Ruth. If you have not, I will disown you, and you will not inherit a cent. You have two hours to make that decision. By the way, Ruth," and she spoke to the trembling girl for the first time. "I will give you $5,000 to divorce my son. That is a great deal of money for you. Think it over."

Ruth said the first word she had spoken since she left Bridget in the entrance. "No!" burst forth from her.

"Well, I won't give you any more than that. We aren't going to, uh, bargain in this instance, Ruth," she said curtly. Then Mrs. Stratton abruptly left the room. As she closed the door quietly behind her and stood for a moment in the twilight, she realized that the fog had come in and it was chilly. She wondered about returning for her coat and then decided against it She had made her exit, and as far as she was concerned, it was a good one. Besides, it would be nice and warm in the car.

She still couldn't believe that Michael had done this to her. It was simply incredible. She was certain, however, that, even if he did not come to his senses, that the little fortune hunter would take the $5,000, once she realized that was the only offer she would get. She had to leave them alone to decide for themselves, but she felt confident that the right decision, with her help, would be forthcoming.

As she walked briskly toward the garage, she noticed the convertible, its top up, sitting in front of the house. Why should she go all the way to the garage when she could take the Chrysler. She still had the key in her purse. And if it would inconvenience them while she was at the Club, so much the better. She strode purposefully to the convertible, got in, and started the motor.

CHAPTER 30

Both Michael and Ruth had remained standing hand-in-hand, frozen by the viciousness of the attack, for some seconds after Mary Stratton had left the house. Michael was the first to recover. He took Ruth in his arms, protectively cradling the small figure.

"I'm so sorry, honey, so sorry," and his handsome face was contorted with helpless rage and grief. "So sorry." That was all he could think of to say.

Ruth was still trembling. She had never been exposed to that kind of abuse, or such blatant bigotry, before.

"Sweetheart," he was still trying to calm her. "You know I love you. You know that I wanted to marry you." And then he burst out with even more words that she desperately needed to hear. "And you know I didn't give up a damn thing to marry you! All I want out of life is life with you, Ruth. And believe me, if any career I might have would be affected because you're Jewish, I'll just choose another career that has nicer people in it!"

"Are you sure?" she whispered, looking up uncertainly at him. "But what if you like the career that has the prejudiced people?" They really weren't making much sense, either of them. But they were communicating love, which was most important to both of them.

"I just wouldn't," he soothed her. "What hurts you, hurts me, sweetheart." He suddenly realized that he had just uttered an exact truth. In fact, he was actually more hurt at what his mother had said to Ruth and about Ruth than what she had said to him. His arms tightened around her.

"Michael," she murmured against his chest. "That was such a terrible thing to offer money to give you up. You know I—" and she couldn't stop the tears running down her face.

"I know, I know," Michael comforted her. "Well, I guess we might as well leave. I can never come back here. She has cut off any ties between us. I'll have to tell Bridget. At least we can keep contact with her, and close contact if I know Bridget."

Ruth had a flash of insight. "It must have been Bridget who raised you, right, Michael? How else could you have grown up into such a wonderful person if—" and she was interrupted by a square figure hurtling herself into the room, not seeming to know whether to embrace Ruth or Michael first and trying to embrace both of them at once. Bridget had waited as long as she deemed discrete, but she could wait no longer.

All three shed a few tears in the midst of the hugs and kisses, and soon love had replaced the venom in that room.

Ruth finally looked around. "You have a lovely home, Michael. I never noticed before." She was glad she hadn't noticed, for she was sure she would have been intimidated by its grandeur if she had. She had had enough of intimidation. Besides, she thought critically, some of the furniture was a little heavy and gloomy. She would have preferred a bit more cheerfulness. Not that it mattered. She was never going to enter this house again.

Michael decided to pack his belongings immediately so that he wouldn't have to return, either. He would have to put it all in his car, all his civilian clothes, the residue of his childhood. He and Ruth would begin looking for an apartment tomorrow that they could move into as soon as they were officially married in the eyes of the family and then he would bring it all to the apartment. Now his mother would finally realize that he would never change his mind. He thought bitterly that she was forcing him into this action.

Ruth helped him pack, exclaiming over some of the more luxurious items, such as the gold watch that he never wore in the Navy. He wore a silver one, a Mido that he liked better. When she found out that he intended to keep everything in the car, she protested that he could put it all in her parents' flat for the short time before they found an apartment. Certainly it would be crowded, but she could stuff it all in her room and close the door.

"Michael," she had been bothered by another statement by Mrs. Stratton that she decided to ask him about.

"Yes, honey?" He was throwing jackets, trousers, and shirts into a cardboard box, while Ruth was taking them out and folding them out before replacing them. He wasn't taking any of his mother's luggage. He wasn't taking anything of his mother's.

"Who was it that advised your mother to give you up for adoption when your father died?" She could hardly say the words.

"Oh, I think it was her aunt, my grandmother's sister. My great-aunt Elizabeth was a very strong lady and liked to tell everyone else what to do. My mother always prides herself on the fact that she kept me even though she was advised against it. But my mother seldom does what anyone tells her to do, anyway," he added.

Ruth was still shocked. She finally came out with, "Well, I think it was just terrible to even consider giving up your own child," and she let it go at that. She would have stolen and possibly even killed to keep her child, if she had one.

"Let's take this stuff out to the car. I don't know if everything is going to fit," Michael suggested. He led the way, carrying what he could with Ruth following with an armload, too.

"Careful of the stairs, honey," he called back to her. And then he opened the front door, checking the blackout curtain that prevented the light from spilling into the street. Ruth, just behind him, closed the door for the same reason. They looked at the empty street in front of the house.

"Wait a minute. Didn't we park right in front?"

Ruth put down her boxes and looked. "Yes, I'm certain we did. Where's the car?"

As Ruth stood there, she was seized by a premonition of danger. She began shaking uncontrollably, out of all proportion to the loss of the car. The very street seemed menacing. She tried to regain control of herself, hoping Michael wouldn't notice, telling herself it was still a reaction to that terrible confrontation with Mrs. Stratton.

Fortunately, Michael was much too preoccupied with this new crisis to notice. He dropped the boxes and limped down the stairs, looking carefully up and down the street. Even with the blackout, he could easily make out the shapes of the few cars on the block, and his convertible was not among them. What the hell! Did someone steal it? Or did Mother . . .

It was just then that a police car rolled up in front of the house and stopped.

CHAPTER 31

Ruth and Michael couldn't believe it. After identifying Michael as Mrs. Stratton's son, he told them that there had been a terrible accident and that Mrs. Stratton was already in an ambulance on the way to the hospital.

The officer was as empathetic as he could be. "I'm sorry, son," he said to Michael, and offered to give them a ride there. They hastily put the boxes inside the front door and let Bridget know they were leaving, and in what seemed like a timeless whirl, were on their way in the squad car, the siren blaring.

Mrs. Stratton was in bad shape. In addition to three broken ribs, she had a severe concussion, though no internal injuries. The doctors assured them that under the circumstances, she was very lucky. The car was totaled. Mrs. Stratton had never seen the truck that sideswiped her in the intersection.

Michael and Ruth stood by helplessly as what seemed like a small army of nurses and technicians tended to his mother. Tubes and monitors seemed to cover her body and it seemed to Michael that the once imposing woman now seemed horribly frail and vulnerable. "We're moving her to intensive care," the doctor informed them. They followed the gurney up to the private room, where they soon settled into a routine of nurses and orderlies and doctors throughout the night.

Ruth had called her parents to let them know about the accident. She and Michael found a few chairs and pushed them together to form a somewhat comfortable settee and it was there, covered with some hospital blankets, that they spent a most miserable and anxious night, half dozing, half still in shock from the night before.

When morning came, his mother's status remained the same. She was woozy and dazed from the concussion, but opened her eyes. Michael darted to her side. "Mother, Mother, it's Michael. You've had a terrible accident, but you're going to be okay." Without warning, tears splashed from his eyes. She was his mother, after all, and he would never wish any harm to come to her.

"Michael," she murmured. "My son . . ."

Ruth felt the same sense of sadness. Despite the horror of the night before, her heart went out to Mrs. Stratton. She leaned near her from the other side of the bed and put her hand gently on her mother-in-law's shoulder. Mary Stratton tried to turn her head in her direction but her son restrained her.

"You must stay still, Mother. Just rest." Just then, a nurse arrived to take her vitals and Ruth and Michael went back to their chairs.

"Why don't you two go and have some breakfast," the nurse advised them. "We'll be taking her for more X-rays in a few minutes and it will be awhile."

Ruth and Michael got up, relieved to have an excuse to leave Mary Stratton's side. They were both disheveled and in desperate need of some sleep themselves, but some toast and ham and eggs and two large cups of coffee seemed to revive them somewhat.

"We've got to make some phone calls," Michael realized. "My aunt and uncle will need to know, as will Bridget and Annie and Joe."

"I'll call Bridget," Ruth offered. "You can get in touch with the others. We'll need some fresh clothes and things if we're to stay here much longer. And I'll need to call work and let them know I won't be there for awhile."

Michael looked at Ruth with an even deeper gaze of love, if that were possible. "Ruth, there's no sense in both of us having to be here night and day."

"Nonsense," she insisted. "You're my husband, and I am going to be right here with you, no matter what!" And with that, they both set out to make arrangements for this new and very strange twist to their first few days as a married couple.

* * *

Catherine Stratton hung up the telephone in her brownstone in New York and sat still for a moment, shocked. And then she cried. She didn't know why she was crying. She had never liked the woman. But she couldn't deny the sorrow she felt, for whatever reason. Perhaps she felt sorry for this latest turn of events for Michael and his new bride. Wiping her eyes, she went to tell her husband, Bill.

At the other end of the phone, Michael sat a few moments longer, wondering who else he should call. Annie and Joe and Bridget had all been informed as had Ruth's parents, who had sent over a change of clothes for Ruth. Mrs. Kaminsky stopped by with a picnic basket full of food for them. Michael realized then that there were very few people whom his mother could call close friends. For that, he felt a wave of sadness wash over him. It was a lonely life his mother led, he thought. That was the price of being so judgmental, so closed up in her emotions.

Close to a week had passed. After careful

observation, the concussion turned out to be not as serious as the doctors had first thought. She would need rest and care for several weeks, but she would be as good as new before long. The broken ribs were going to be painful for quite some time, but they, too, would heal.

When Mary was a bit more rested, she called Michael over to her bedside and took his hand. "You've been here all this time," she marveled. "Of course, Mother, and so has Ruth." At the mention of Ruth's name, Mrs. Stratton grimaced. "Ruth, yes."

Ruth tentatively brushed some of the hair out of Mrs. Stratton's eyes. "Mrs. Stratton, I am so glad that you are okay. We've been so worried about you." For the first time, Ruth looked directly into Mrs. Stratton's blue eyes. They seemed old and faded, but sparkled in the same way that Michael's did. What Mrs. Stratton said next surprised her.

"You have been an angel, my dear. Thank you. Would you mind if I had a few minutes alone with Michael?"

"Of course," Ruth agreed. "I'll go get some coffee."

When she left the room, Mrs. Stratton grasped her son's hand more firmly. "Michael, I want you to know . . . that I've been wrong."

Michael was taken aback. "Mother, you don't need to . . ."

"Now listen to me, Michael. I know this sounds cliché, but when I was hit by that truck, something happened. I saw my entire life flash before me, but it was more than that. It was like I went back in time and I remembered what it was like when you were born and how happy I was that you had come into this world. When your father died so soon after, something died with me. I didn't know what to do or who to turn to. It seemed like the whole world was against me."

She pressed his hand more tightly. "You and your happiness were the only thing that mattered to me. And it is still true. I want you to be happy. And if it is Ruth that will make you happy, then I will just have to accept that."

Michael was overwhelmed by this complete turnabout by his mother. He really didn't quite believe it, and for a moment even wondered if she were trying to trick him. But she continued on.

"I want you two to have a real wedding. And I want you to do this soon, so that I can be there, too, and wish you well. It's important to me."

"Oh, Mother, that would mean so much to us!" Michael exclaimed. "We have hoped that you would change your mind and this is like the answer to our prayers."

* * *

Ruth felt a stab of guilt as she took the elevator down to the cafeteria. It was probably her fault that Mrs. Stratton never liked her. She knew that, if she had behaved with more propriety and dressed more conservatively at the USO, she wouldn't have antagonized her so; but, contrary to good manners and good sense, she had flaunted herself, and even challenged the older woman—and lost. Ruth hid her face in her hands, appalled by her own behavior. She had even hoped, for a horrifying moment when she first heard about the accident, that Mrs. Stratton was dead. It would have solved all their problems. The thought of this made Ruth feel even more remorseful. What a terrible person I am to have thought that! This was the woman that was Michael's mother and for good or bad, she was now her family.

So Ruth was a bit shocked to return to the hospital room and to be greeted with smiles by both Michael and Mrs. Stratton.

"Ruth, my Mother has something to tell you," Michael said, leading her over to the bed. Mrs. Stratton was propped up and she extended both her hands to Ruth and pulled her near.

"Ruth, I have just finished telling Michael that I want you both to have a beautiful wedding." Mrs. Stratton saw the incredulous look on Ruth's face and continued. "I know this is shocking, but I had an extraordinary experience during my accident." She paused and took a deep breath. "Ruth, I want you to forgive me for my cold actions toward you. I want you to forgive me for my comments about your reputation and your religion. I hope that you will forgive me for all these things. I want you and Michael to be happy and I want to do everything I can to help you both."

At that, Ruth burst into tears and it wasn't long before Michael and Mrs. Stratton joined her. One of the doctors walked in.

"I'm sorry to interrupt this family reunion," he said. "But Mrs. Stratton, we'll be releasing you this morning. It's time now to be going home."

CHAPTER 32

Ruth was every bit as excited about this wedding as she was about her first. It was a cold clear day in November. The fog, a San Francisco trademark, seemed to have lifted just for them. She gazed at herself in the mirror in her bedroom in her borrowed finery, wishing she could have afforded a new wedding gown, but glad that Mrs. Kaminsky had loaned her hers as part of the "something old, something new, something borrowed, something blue" that tradition called for. Michael had pleaded to be allowed to buy one for Ruth, but he was firmly told that it "wasn't your place to buy that, honey," and he had to be satisfied with engaging the best photographer and buying the best flowers in the city. White orchids were everywhere, not only decorating the house, but on the shoulders of every woman who attended. Ruth's bouquet was a dream of white orchids, spray of lily-of-the-valley and bouvardia, and Sally, as her Maid of Honor, carried the orchids mixed with yellow roses and wore a matching crown of blossoms, which were the exact shade of her pale yellow taffeta gown.

Ruth's old-fashioned gown was lovely, made of white satin with a tight-fitting bodice, long pointed sleeves, full skirt and a long train. For "something new," Ruth wore a fingertip veil of French lace and illusion, which was fastened to a seed pearl and sequin crown. After Mrs. Braunstein had used a needle to good effect here and there, the gown fit perfectly, and Mrs. Kaminsky had crowed with delight when she saw her in it. It seemed as if it had been created for the small girl with the shining red hair.

Catherine and Bill arrived and had insisted on hosting the rehearsal dinner at the elegant Claremont Hotel in Berkeley across the San Francisco Bay, which they had all enjoyed tremendously. Uncle Bill would stand up for Michael as best man, in place of Pete, who was still on assignment in New Caledonia. Pete and Rita, now married, had argued over what to send them for their wedding, Rita hoping for a more conventional gift. They finally sent them a long letter along with a special package. When Ruth and Michael unwrapped it, they both practically fell over laughing. It was a large wooden hand-carved statue of a woman with long hair down her back. The way you could tell it was a woman was by her large, pointed breasts, which dominated the entire figure. Pete knew Mike would appreciate this. Pete didn't know if it was a fertility symbol or not, but it had been carved by the native Noumeans and he felt it would bring them luck.

She heard the strains of the Wedding March on the old Victrola through the closed door and knew that it was time. As she prepared to leave her childhood bedroom, she thought again of her brother, Jerry, and her eyes filled with tears. He would have been so happy for her. She wiped her eyes hastily on the back of her hand and gave a last look around at all the wedding gifts—the beautiful English wedding china they had picked out and all the boxes tied up with pretty paper and silver ribbons. She opened the door, almost bumping into her father and Sally, who were hurrying to fetch her. Excited and nervous in his rented tuxedo and with a perky carnation in his buttonhole, Max whispered, "It's time, Ruth, it's time." He had practiced the special hesitation steps he was supposed to take over and over, but he still didn't have them right. Sally, looking absolutely lovely, smiled at Ruth and took her place behind her.

They marched out of Ruth's room, by the kitchen, where corned beef, sliced turkey, breads, salads, champagne, schnapps, fruit punch for the children, and a magnificent wedding cake with a crown of a sailor and his bride were spread upon the table, and into the front room, decorated with more orchids than guests, where everyone was assembled.

As the lovely bride passed Mrs. Kaminsky, she turned to her husband, proud that her gown could be used again to bring her friend happiness, and she whispered that Ruth was much more beautiful than she ever was. Mr. Kaminsky whispered back that he didn't think so at all, although of course Ruth was a beautiful bride, and they smiled at each other. She was glad that she didn't feel that terrible sense of foreboding at all anymore. All she could see in the future now for Ruth was happiness.

Ruth smiled upon her weeping mother, looking quite handsome in a new aqua lace gown with a white orchid pinned to it; upon the Kaminskys who were seated next to Mrs. Stratton, who looked especially elegant; upon her brother David and her sister-in-law Debbie and their two adorable daughters; upon Aunt Catherine, upon Sally's parents, Mr. and Mrs. Simpson and their two younger children; upon Bridget, crying happily and sitting with Annie and Joe; upon her friends and Michael's friends and her parent's friends, as the small procession made its way up to the minister. There, Michael, looking so handsome in his uniform that she could hardly stand it, was waiting with Uncle Bill, replete in an elegant tuxedo, complete with carnation.

Michael watched her with his heart in his eyes, thinking he had never seen anyone more beautiful. Her eyes and Michael's met, and their lives truly began.

EPILOGUE

Jerry Stratton banged on his high chair with his spoon and beamed, saying what might have been "cake" with his mouth full of the confection. It was August 14, 1945 and their son was one year old today. Ruth and Michael smiled at one another. Life was great. It was a joy being together, and Jerry, named after the uncle he would never know, was what Mother Braunstein called a "mitzvah," a blessing. He was such a blessing that they planned to have another baby in about a year.

Ruth, particularly, thanked God every day, not only for the fact that she could have a "normal" life, but that she was able to have babies and look after the modest house she and Michael had built in Oakland and spend five hours a day at her volunteer work, despite what the doctors had said; but also because Michael had been permanently (or as permanently as the war permitted) assigned to the Alameda Naval Base, where he was safe. He even came home every night almost as if everything were normal again.

She had spent her day as usual, rolling bandages and helping the nurses, but the hardest part of it had been, as usual, tending the mortally and critically wounded men. She'd often thought of what it must have been like for Michael when he'd been wounded so far from home. Although neither had gone into detail, they had both long ago confessed to each other that they'd had attractions to others while they'd been apart, but that their love for one another was greater than anything in their pasts. She smiled at Sally across the table, who wished that she could have volunteered as a Gray Lady for the Red Cross, too. Just last week, she finally admitted that she and Harry were "sort of engaged" and she simultaneously stopped going to the USO and the Hop House. Sally's new job at the shipyards took all her time and that, too, helped the war effort as well as Sally's pocketbook.

This damn war! It was never-ending. She had thought that on May 8th, when Germany surrendered, that Japan would follow suit immediately, but they didn't. We were forced to unleash that terrible weapon, the Atom Bomb, on the Japanese. She shuddered. There were rumors that it could cause vibrations that could actually destroy the world! She clung to the thought that at least if it finally caused the Japanese to surrender, it would save countless American lives. She had helped, or tried to help, too many of them.

Mary Stratton hurried to Jerry and wiped some of the frosting from his sticky hands and face. It wasn't necessary to feed him the cake. He was doing very well himself, but spoons were apparently only for banging, as far as he was concerned. Mary seemed to take particular joy in her grandson. Although Ruth realized that her caustic personality would never change, she was like a different person when she was around little Jerry. Ruth didn't know what she would do without her or Bridget, who were always willing to step in and help out when she needed them. She wouldn't have been able to help out at the hospital as she had been doing without them, certainly. She had tendered her resignation to The White House as soon as she'd found out she was pregnant, as the doctor had ordered and although she did have a bit of trouble carrying the baby, there were absolutely no complications at birth. Pete and Rita's fertility symbol seemed to have rubbed off on all of them, as they had just announced that Rita was expecting. She dusted the wooden statue, which had a place of honor on their bedroom bureau, almost every day.

She remembered how shocked Pete was when he was finally convinced of Rita's true background. He wrote that he didn't even speak to Rita for two days, which was silly, for she had never deceived him—he had just refused to believe the truth. Then he got on his high horse and insisted on continuing his plans to become a doctor through the G.I. Bill and that he wouldn't accept any help from her family. That was truly a wonderful bill they had passed last year, paying married veterans $90 a month while they attended college.

She reminded herself that she owed a letter to Aunt Catherine and Uncle Bill. Such wonderful people! She was delighted, too, at the way Mrs. Kaminsky and her mother now had something in common—little Jerry. There seemed to be no jealousy left between them. Mrs. Kaminsky had also become a special friend to Mary Stratton. Although they clearly were from different worlds, they shared Mrs. Stratton's growing interest in all things paranormal and to everyone's surprise Mary proved to be an enthusiastic and talented student of psychometry.

Ruth looked around the room. She loved everyone at the table, her family, her friends. Her father was the epitome of the patriarch, while David and Debbie's girls were like little mothers to Jerry, who loved it. Ruth was ecstatic that she had married Michael. All that was needed now was for the war to end.

The radio played softly in the background and when she heard "When the Lights Go On Again" she wished with all her heart that the words would come true, that the lights <u>would</u> go on again all over the world, that there would be no more blackouts, no more killing, no more ward that would bloody the planet. And then, there was an interruption by the announcer. Everyone stopped talking, even the baby, and listened intently. The Japanese had surrendered. The war was over, finally over.

And then, there was a time of peace.

ABOUT THE AUTHOR

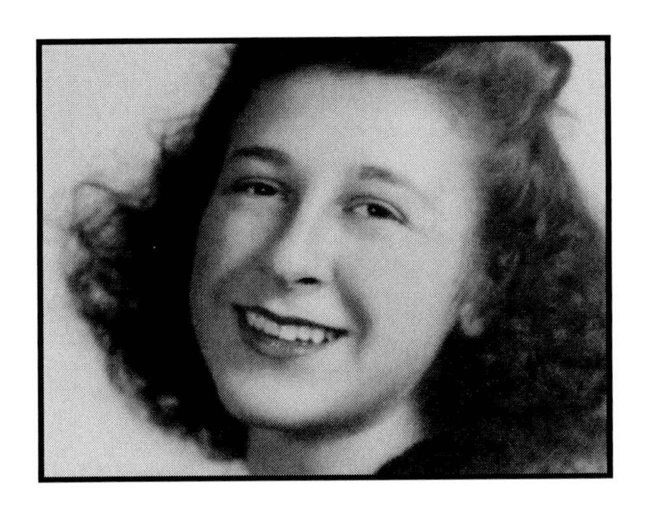

From the beginning, there was something different about Florence Gold. She was born on August 20,1924 with a rheumatic heart in San Francisco, California. She was not expected to live, but an optimistic doctor, for whom she was later named, encouraged her parents to give the struggling infant a chance.

That optimism set the tone for Florence's entire life. She was known by all as one of the most genuine, kind and positive people they would ever meet. She believed that, "If you believed in the best, the best would happen." Her faith in the goodness of life served to inspire and comfort her friends and family, even during very difficult times.

Florence always spoke from the heart and was sincerely interested in others. She was a mentor and touchstone for many young people, including her son, Stephen and her daughter, Diane. She and her husband, Robert Gold, have been described as, "the happiest, most devoted two people in the world."

Florence graduated from Burlingame High School and studied English at San Francisco City College. Her love of literature and learning continued throughout her life. Her many travels brought her to Europe, Australia, New Zealand, Fiji and on many occasions, Maui, Hawaii, where she and Robert always celebrated their anniversary.

Although Florence passed away on April 20, 2011, she continues to be a powerful, inspiring presence. This novel, set in WWII, speaks of a more innocent time, but tells a universal story of the value of unconditional love and forgiveness—the very things that Florence trusted in and practiced throughout her own life.

Azalea Art Press
specializes in giving personal attention
to authors who wish to realize
their literary and creative dreams.

To learn more about writing and creating
your next print or e-book, please visit:

AzaleaArtPress.blogspot.com

To order more copies of
this novel by Florence Gold
please email the publisher at
azaleaartpress@gmail.com

or visit www.lulu.com